Lots of times lately I think about Mr. Desnick when I'm running. One story I like to imagine is what would happen if there was a huge snowstorm one day at the end of school, after all the buses were gone, and if I was the last person to come back from running cross-country.

Mr. Desnick would be in the field house when I come in, and we would be the only people left in the building. The snow would be so high by then that we couldn't leave the field house, and all the telephone lines would be down and the electricity, too, would go out at some point.

In the story we have to spend the whole night together talking in the field house. And because it gets very cold in the middle of the night— there's also no heat because of the snowstorm —we have to hold each other to keep warm. And then we start kissing, of course. Oh, I'd also have some Almond Joys in my locker so we could eat them instead of real food, cause there wouldn't be any, when we get hungry.

FOOTFALLS

Elizabeth Harlan

FAWCETT JUNIPER • NEW YORK

RLI: $\dfrac{\text{VL: } 6 + \text{up}}{\text{IL: } 9 + \text{up}}$

A Fawcett Juniper Book
Published by Ballantine Books
Copyright © 1982 by Elizabeth Harlan

Library of Congress Catalog Card Number: 82-6727

ISBN 0-449-70074-7

This edition published by arrangement with Atheneum

Manufactured in the United States of America

First Ballantine Books Edition: January 1984

For my father with love remembered
For thou art with me

One

I'm running more now. And faster. I was running just three miles a day before school started, but now I'm up to five and six miles, and sometimes, like yesterday morning, when the air is just right and my body feels good, I even run eight or ten miles lately.

Our pediatrician Dr. Gilbert told Mom at my checkup last year that too much distance running might not be good for me. He told her some girls who exercise too hard don't get their period when they should. But I got mine in August, and even if Mom doesn't approve, I plan to run as fast and as far as I can. Some day I intend to be a marathon racer like the Norwegian runner, Grete Waitz.

People have even said I look like her when I run, cause my hair is long and lightish brown like hers, and I have very long legs. Also, Grete Waitz has a slightly too-big nose, and so do I.

I like my Adidas TrX Competition running shoes better than my Nikes. The problem is, Nike makes the Road Runner for girls in a yucky light blue color, which gets dirty the minute you wear them. The men's Road Runner is a really nice dark blue. I hate it when they make the women's running shoes one color and the men's another. And then they call the women's shoes names like "Lady Brooks." I thought they weren't supposed to call females "ladies" anymore. You'd think that'd be especially true for female athletes.

In fact, lots of people still think being athletic is really for boys, but they're wrong, of course. Mom's that way. She couldn't care less that I made varsity track this fall, which means I'm one of the seven girls on the team who get to run at all the meets. The other kids only run if they need an extra when one of us is out, or for practice so they'll get better. I'm the only freshman who made varsity.

Mom thinks getting good grades is more important than making a team. Whenever I tell her I'll be home late from school cause of practice, she always looks mad and asks if I'll have enough time to get my homework done.

Mom never finished college cause she married Daddy after sophomore year. She was studying art history and was about to go on a junior year in Rome, but when Daddy proposed she decided to get married instead.

I'm sure Mom's sorry now that she never went on her junior year abroad or finished college, and I'm sure that's why she's on my back all the time about studying and getting good grades.

Besides, Mom's the most unathletic person in the world—or almost. She does play tennis every week with her friends, but they're all oldish and a little overweight like Mom. You can tell they really care more about talking to each other than tennis or exercise, cause whenever I've seen them play they can never even keep track of the score.

I think I did a full ten miles yesterday, which would be a first. I wish I was old enough to drive a car, so I could go out and clock how many miles I run. Mom never has time when I ask her if she'll do it with me. And by the time Daddy gets home, it's too dark already.

Daddy commutes by train to New York City every day, where he does market research for a big company that makes things like hairspray and hand lotion. His job is to find out what people who buy the stuff really want, so the company can make better products that more people will buy. Lots of times Daddy brings home samples for Mom and me to try.

Daddy's very idealistic about his work and believes market researchers have a responsibility to make products healthy and safe for the people who use them. Lots of times Daddy comes home all hassled about arguments he has with his boss, Mr. Frye, who cares lots less about health and safety than he does about making lots of money.

When I was a little girl and Daddy took me to his office for the first time, I was too young to know what a market researcher was. When I got home I told everyone that my father was a telephone operator, cause he spent the whole day talking on the phone. For a real long time afterwards, Daddy used to tell people the story, and everyone always laughed when he told it.

Daddy gets tired a lot easier lately. Since the operation last winter when they took a growth off his back, he seems older in a lot of ways. Mom says it'll just take time, but sometimes I think he's getting worse not better.

He said he'd clock mileage with me this weekend, but I know by the time he gets through taking my brother Robby to ice hockey practice on Saturday and then to the game on Sunday, he'll say he's beat and doesn't feel like it.

It's not really fair that Daddy watches Robby's games all the time *and* drives him all over creation to get there, but no one has time to clock mileage for my running. I think Daddy cares more about Robby's sports than he does about mine.

But I don't really care that no one ever watches me run cross-country. Runners are supposedly very self-sufficient people. They can also stand a lot more pain and stress than most athletes. And anyway, I think part of why I love running so much is cause it gives me a chance to be off by myself in the woods and in my own head where no one can get to me.

Yesterday morning was absolute perfection. Cool but not cold, at least not once I got warmed up after the first mile or so, and I loved the sound of running on crunchy piles of leaves. I was thinking the whole time that the woods were a wilderness and that mine were the first human feet to fall on those leaves. Something kept buzzing in my head about fallen leaves and "footfalls," but I'm not sure if that's a real word.

The ground beneath my feet reminded me of those collages we used to make in art class with little specks of red and orange and yellow construction paper glued with milky white glue to a piece of cardboard. Then we'd all print something like "Fall Leaves" at the top and bring it home to show our mothers. I wonder if Mom threw away all that stuff I made in elementary school.

The other neat thing about yesterday's run was the way I felt when I got home. It was still only seven fifteen, cause I set my alarm to get up really early so I could run for a long time. It was dark out when I left, and I ran right straight into sunrise, which was beautiful.

When I came in the back door I was very excited about how far I'd run, and everyone was already sitting around the table having cereal, so it was kind of like crossing a finish line with spectators on the sidelines.

"How far'd you go, Babes?" Dad asked, and when I told him I thought I'd done about ten, everyone looked really impressed, and even snotty Robby said, "Wow!" Robby's twelve going on two, and he's in seventh grade. He's a real creep.

The good feeling about the run didn't last long, cause when I sat down to have breakfast Mom said, "Go wash up before coming to the table, Stephanie." Stephanie's my full name, but everyone who knows me calls me Stevie. Except people like teachers and my mother. She says Stevie's not a girl's name and that she likes the name she gave me better. But I don't.

Mom was probably annoyed that I got up early to run. She's a real nut about my getting enough sleep. And I'm sure she didn't think it was good for me to run that far, which I'll probably hear about some other time. I told her I washed before running, and she snapped at me that washing two hours ago doesn't count and not to be fresh.

I also think she was upset about Dad, who was talking about maybe not going in to work that day cause he didn't feel very good. That kind of took the afterglow out of the morning. From then on everything was just the way it usually is—an ordinary, not so great school morning.

.   .   .

6

When I got to the corner where Jenny was waiting to meet me, I remembered I forgot the book on the Civil War that I needed for my history term paper. I have a two-hour study hall on Thursday afternoons, and I was planning to work on a section of the paper that needed background material from the book.

I almost decided not to go back for it, cause it meant walking alone and getting to school very late. But then Jenny said she'd come with me, so we went back to my house together.

"The thing that really gets to me," I was explaining on the way back to Jenny, who's also on the track team, "is that even though I can run all those miles, I have no way of figuring out how many miles I've gone. I hate depending on adults all the time. You can never rely on them."

"My mom's reliable," Jenny answered. "And that's worse. She just waits around for me to find things for her to do. She always wants to help me plan parties or something, and she and Dad always want me to go places and do things with them, instead of staying home by myself."

I told Jenny, "That's 'cause you're the youngest," but as I said it, I didn't really believe Mom would be different if I *were* the baby in the family. I'm sure Robby'd still be her favorite.

As we got to the back door I heard Mom talking to someone, and then I remembered that Daddy was staying home from work. But when I came in the kitchen I saw Mom was in there alone, and she was talking on the phone, not to Daddy. She was telling someone—I figured it must be one of her tennis partners—that she couldn't play today cause Phil was home sick.

It sort of surprised me that Mom would give up her tennis game because Daddy didn't feel well. Whenever I have a virus or anything and stay home, Mom just leaves for a couple of hours and plays tennis anyway. And Daddy didn't even really look that sick at breakfast.

When Mom saw me and Jenny come in, she looked kind of annoyed. She finished her conversation and hung up the phone before she said anything to us, and all she said then was, "Leave something behind, Stephanie? Oh hi, Jenny." And off she went up the back stairs.

Times like that embarrass me in front of my friends, cause their mothers are always so much nicer and more interested in me than Mom is in my friends. But Jenny didn't seem to notice.

It surprised me that the breakfast dishes were all still on the table. Even the milk carton wasn't put back in the refrigerator. Usually, Mom has this thing about cleaning up.

Just as we were going out the back door, I heard Mom call out in a really weird-sounding voice, "Phil, are you all right? What is it, Phil?" And then I heard the retching sounds people make when they're throwing up. Jenny was already down the steps by then, and I didn't think she heard anything, so I just pretended everything was OK and left. I guess I was embarrassed that Jenny might find out Daddy was sick and throwing up.

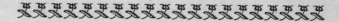

Two

It's Sunday evening now, the end of another weekend, and my term paper on the Civil War is due tomorrow. I still have two parts left to write and the whole thing to type, plus the bibliography. I know I'll be up all night, and I'm already exhausted.

The weekend was a real bummer. Bad weather, so I hardly got to run, and Mom in a lousy mood the whole time, cause she had to drive Robby to hockey all weekend. Daddy's been in bed since Thursday, when he threw up, and even though Mom says it's just a bout of the flu, I'm sure it's more than that.

Every time I picked up the phone all weekend, she barked at me to be quick cause she was expecting an important call. When the call finally came, it turned out it was from Dr. Wechsler, the surgeon who operated on Daddy last winter. You don't have to talk to a surgeon for the flu, so Daddy must be getting sick again like last time.

I kept thinking it'd be nice if I went up to Daddy's room to keep him company for a while, but it's depressing to be around him when he's not feeling well. He just kind of lies there very still, not reading or anything, with his eyes looking out the window at the silver maple. This time of year the tree is bare, so there's really nothing much to see out there.

The one time I was in Daddy's room was on Saturday morning when I went through to get Mom's hair dryer. He held his arm out from the bed as though he wanted to tag me as I went by, but I ignored it, cause I was in a rush to blow my hair out before it dried in waves. I guess I could've at least given him a kiss on the way.

My muscles feel all stiff up the back of my legs. It's cause I didn't get to run this weekend. Earlier this evening I did some warm-up exercises and stretches to try to work out some of the stiffness. I was sitting on the floor looking at myself in the mirror with the soles of my feet pressed together, doing some leg bounces, and I noticed, cause I was wearing just a bra and panties, that my breasts have gotten a lot more developed since the summer.

I could tell because of the way they filled out my

bra and then kind of bulged a little over the top. That never happened in the two-piece I wore swimming all last summer. And the cup sizes are the same.

Sometimes lately when I do bounces like that, I get a tingly feeling deep down, and then I think of the boys' gym teacher, Mr. Desnick. I can't decide if I think it would be nice to have him for a father or a husband. He's very handsome, and I love the way he looks right at you with a really serious gaze when he talks to you.

It makes me nervous to be around him, but I like it when he comes over to watch our track practices. He always seems to care about how you're doing. He's really a very kind man. I have the feeling that if he had a daughter and she needed something from him, he'd be sure to give it to her.

Jenny says her older sister Gwenn thinks he's a lech and that Jenny should keep her distance. I don't really think so, though. That he's a lech, I mean. And I don't believe the rumor the boys started that Joey Robinson and Gregg Myer saw Mr. Desnick kissing Stacy Miller last year in the tunnels under the school building.

Yesterday at track practice I came in with the team's best time for the 3.2 mile cross-country run. I ran it in 19 flat, almost a minute faster than Beth Kile. Since I've been running longer distances, I have much more speed and endurance.

I'm also learning how to pace myself. When you run long distance, you don't let it all out right away like you do when you run just a mile. You have to plan when to put on a spurt, or you'll use up all your energy and wear out too soon.

We were sitting on the steps outside the field house waiting for the last runners to get back from practice, and our coach, Mrs. Mackley, came over and said to me, right in front of the rest of the team, "I think you've got a shot at first place in the 3.2 mile cross-country at East Bradley, Stevie Farr."

She always calls everyone by both their names. If you've been around Mrs. Mackley enough and heard her do that a lot, it stops sounding so strange. Now if she called me just Stevie, without the Farr, that would sound strange.

East Bradley is where the fall running conference for our area is going to be held this year. Wakefield, which is our school, Somerset, Greenboro, and East Bradley are the four high schools in our conference.

I felt really proud and happy when Mrs. Mackley said that, until I looked over at Jenny, who's not even on the varsity yet. She won't be running at East Bradley. I also noticed Beth Kile, who's a senior and who takes a lot of firsts in the 3.2, make eyes at Debbie Seligman. She's a junior who's also on the varsity, but she's so slow it's pathetic. They hang around together a lot and talk about track and running so much you'd think they invented it.

Beth's real affected and always acts like she's

dying after she finishes a race. She kind of limps around with her hands on her hips and does a whole bunch of warm-up exercises and stretches in front of everyone at the finish line. You'd think she just finished under three hours in the Boston Marathon.

Beth and Debbie always act real snotty toward me, but I don't care, cause I know they're just jealous I made varsity as a freshman and they didn't.

Then Mrs. Mackley told us about what the course will be like on the fourteenth at the girls' conference. It goes through the woods and along a canal that runs behind East Bradley High. The course gets bendy and *very* narrow at some places, so passing can be tricky and taking position early in the race and holding on is important.

It's about an hour and a half by bus from our school to East Bradley, so we won't get to run the course ahead of time. Mrs. Mackley said that wouldn't be a disadvantage, cause you always get to walk the course or jog it slowly the morning of the meet, and the route will be marked with people posted all along the way. But I still think it's not fair that the East Bradley kids and the ones from Somerset and Greenboro, who live closer, will all get to run it and we won't.

The conference is a month from now, and Mrs. Mackley is giving each of us a training schedule to keep so we'll be ready by November fourteenth. I'm supposed to run certain set amounts each different day of the week, so someone is going to have to clock distances for me for the days I don't get to run at school. Tonight I'm going to tell Mom that it's a requirement. Then she'll have to help me.

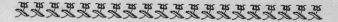

Three

Tonight was an awful night. I wish I could take it back so it would've never happened. Daddy came down to dinner for the first time in a week, and Mom cooked roast beef, which she only does when something special is happening.

Stupid Robby asked why we were having roast beef since tonight was just a Thursday school night, and Mom said, smiling at Daddy, "Because your father's feeling better today." Then dumb Robby blurted out, "You usually save roast beef for special things."

Mom overreacted, the way she always does when Robby acts negative like that, and screamed at him not to be so insensitive. He screamed back and

16

wound up getting sent to his room. Robby's so stupid. He loves roast beef, and he didn't even get to eat any.

It turns out he was in a lousy mood cause he got an F on a math test and had to stay after school to review stuff with his math teacher Mrs. Golomb. Robby hates Mrs. Golomb. Actually, Robby hates school. The only thing he likes is gym and sports. He's a terrible student and has practically no friends, cause he always argues and fights with everyone.

He even had to see the Lower School guidance counselor for a while last year. Mom had to go and pick him up by car at 4:15 on Thursdays, cause his appointment made him miss the school bus. It really embarrasses me to have a brother act the way Robby does. I wish he went to another school.

After Robby went up to his room, I decided to bring up the East Bradley meet and my training schedule. Dad said, "That's neat, Babes," when I told him I made top time for my team in the 3.2 cross-country run, and Mom said, "You must be very proud of yourself, Stephanie."

I never know how to answer that kind of statement. It's not really a question, but it kind of calls for an answer. You can't exactly say, "Yes, I'm very proud of myself," cause that sounds conceited and dumb, and if you say nothing, you sound rude for not answering. I wound up saying nothing, which I could tell by her face Mom interpreted as an insult.

Anyway, I don't believe she really thinks what I did is so special.

Then I hit them with the business about needing to keep a schedule and clocking mileage and so on, but I guess my timing was poor, cause suddenly Mom threw one of her fits. She just took off about how there were other people on this earth besides me and other things to do besides running and that kids had to learn that the universe doesn't revolve around them.

She got so carried away she was practically crying at the same time she was screaming, and then she threw her napkin down on her plate, which was still full of food, and ran out of the room. Which left Daddy and me alone at the table with the roast beef—which suddenly seemed silly, it looked so big.

I felt like crying. Sitting there just Daddy and me on Daddy's first night back at dinner. I felt like I had to make it up to him, but I couldn't figure out what to say or do. I asked him if he was all over his flu, and he said he felt much better. But when I looked at him then, which was about the first time I looked at him during the whole meal, I didn't think he looked good at all. He wasn't very clean-looking, and his hair was oily. His face, which was all pale, didn't look like he'd shaved in a real long time, and his eyes were red and bleary.

It was what he said when I looked at him that made me start to cry. I don't know why, but when Daddy said, "Hey, Stevie, how about you and me going for a drive to clock some miles now?" I just began to bawl like a baby.

We never did get to take that drive. Daddy went upstairs to change while I cleared the table for Mom, but when he came down, he was in the same robe and pajamas he wore at dinner.

I was at the sink scraping food from the plates into the disposal, and Daddy came up to me looking very sad and apologetic. "Mom's really very upset, Babes, and Robby's being temperamental. I just don't think we should leave them like that." He paused for a minute, kind of searching my face for a reaction, and then he said, sounding as tired as I've ever heard him sound, "Anyway, Stevie, I'm beat."

I couldn't help what I said then, even though it was an awful, spoiled-rotten thing to say. But I just kind of lost control and screamed out at him, "You're always beat. Except when it comes to Robby. You always do what he wants you to do, and I can't even get anyone around here to help me with a school requirement!"

I was screaming and crying at the same time by now, just like Mom before. I didn't know what to do with myself I was so angry, and I guess I must've thrown the plate I was scraping into the sink.

Suddenly the disposal was making the worst sounding noises, like glass cracking, and tiny pieces of the white plate were flying up from the sink and into my face. Daddy reached over, pushing me off balance as he did it, to turn the disposal switch off. And when he pushed me, I sort of collapsed against the wall and started sobbing, as though he'd attacked me even though it was just an accident.

Daddy held me then, and I felt all the anger and tears were draining out of me as we hugged each other. The place just beneath the shoulder of his robe was drenched from my running nose and tears. Then Robby came in and saw me crying like a baby, and I couldn't stand facing him, so I ran upstairs to my room where I stayed the entire rest of the night.

As I was falling off to sleep, I thought about Daddy and how tired he looked and how much I love him—much more than I love Mom really—and I could tell I wasn't angry at him anymore. I couldn't help thinking about the ride we almost took.

It would've been nice, the two of us, out at night, quiet, riding around together and talking. Daddy's good to talk with, when he's not tired or sick or anything, cause he talks slowly and listens carefully without acting like you only have fifteen seconds and then he'll have to be off doing something else.

I imagined the car, with its heater kind of vibrating the way it does, and I could see a big, yellow, flat-faced moon in the distance through the windows.

Then I remembered about running the 3.2 mile run in 19 flat, and I thought of Mr. Desnick and tried to imagine how he would act when he heard about it. I imagined him driving by me on my way home from school and stopping to congratulate me and then offering me a lift.

I pictured me and Mr. Desnick driving in his car, with us sitting close enough so his leg was touching mine. I got that tingling feeling deep down again, and I put my hand on the inside of my leg and rubbed a little. Only I was pretending it was Mr. Desnick's hand. Then I moved the hand all around and rubbed harder, which felt really good. I wonder if I'm falling in love.

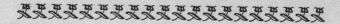

Four

My birthday is this Friday, October thirtieth. I'll be fourteen. That sounds old. My party was going to be a trip to Radio City Music Hall in New York this year, but since Daddy's been in bed sick again, Mom said we had to plan something closer to home. So I'm having a slumber party here with six friends—Jenny, Rachel, Samantha, Alyn, Carol, and Margo.

Margo's my best friend from the summer swim team; and even though she doesn't go to Wakefield School, where I go, she knows all the kids coming to the party from around.

Everyone who's coming likes her except Sammy, and that's cause Sammy's mother works in the same real estate office as Margo's mother and says Mrs. Cotton (Margo's mom) is very competitive and steals other people's commissions. Which is a pretty dumb reason not to like Margo, who has nothing to do with that anyway. I would've invited Meaghan, but Mom said six plus me was the limit.

Since my party will be the night before Halloween, and we're all too old for trick or treating, we're making it a kind of costume slumber party, but all the costumes have to be very movie starish types of costumes. Everyone agreed to that since no one wants to dress up like a ballerina or a clown anymore.

Mom said I could use her black nightgown with the rhinestones on the straps (*if* I was careful), and I'm going to buy a cheap wig somewhere and wear lots of eye makeup and dark red, very long, fake fingernails. Jenny's going to make her nails silver with lavender half-moons, but I think that's too tacky.

About Mom's nightgown with rhinestones on the straps. I've only seen her wear it once in a while. Usually she wears pajamas or a flannel nightie.

When we went to Bermuda two years ago and Robby and I had a room that connected to Mom's and Daddy's at the hotel where we stayed, I remember walking in their room in the morning and seeing the rhinestone nightie on the floor by Mom's side of the bed. At the time I thought it was strange for Mom to take her nightie off while she was sleeping. God, was I immature then! It's still kind of hard to imagine my own parents really having sex together.

The plan for my party is that we're having pizza at the house for dinner first. We decided everyone will bring the costume stuff in bags and leave it upstairs in my room 'til after dinner, cause eating pizza and dressing up like movie stars don't really go together. And then for our party activity we'll get dressed up and help each other with makeup and everything.

Daddy said we could borrow his Polaroid to take pictures. And he didn't even say, "If you're careful." At first he offered to take pictures for us, but I thought we'd feel too self-conscious. Especially the other kids in front of someone else's father. So Daddy showed me how to use the camera myself.

I told Mom I wanted Robby to make plans to be away that night. She said it was his home too and that was up to him, but that she would suggest it. What she really meant was that he's so unpopular no one would want him to stay at their house overnight, so he'll probably wind up being home. Ugh!

At track practice yesterday Mrs. Mackley told us that if the girls who are running cross-country at East Bradley get permission slips from their parents, we can ride to East Bradley with the boys' team this Saturday when they have their meet. That way we'll have a chance to run the course before the fourteenth.

I'm definitely going, even though I know I'll be very tired from my party the night before. I already got my permission slip and signed up for the bus. It'll take the whole day, but it should be fun and worth it.

The only thing I'll have to miss is a shopping trip to the mall with Mom to choose my birthday present. I want clothes this year. But she said we could do it one evening during the week.

We can't do it Sunday, cause Grandma and Papa-La are coming for lunch. Papa-La is what we call our grandfather. We've always called him that. His real name is Lawrence, and Grandma calls him La, pronounced Lah, so we just naturally started calling him Papa-La when we were little.

Since Papa-La turned seventy and doesn't see as well as he used to, they come for lunch instead of dinner so they can drive back and forth in daylight. Mom cooks an enormous lunch with meat and vegetables and everything when they come and calls it Sunday dinner. We never eat like that at lunch any other time. Then for dinner, when they leave, we wind up eating something like eggs, which we never usually eat except at breakfast, and the whole day feels all confused.

Papa-La retired two years ago when he was sixty-eight. That was when he sold his bakery on Hudson Street in Trenton, which he owned for forty-three years. He used to work twelve hours every day but Sundays. Lots of restaurants all over

New Jersey and even some in New York bought bread from Papa-La's bakery.

When he sold his bakery, he also sold the yeast culture that his famous rye bread and salt sticks were made from. The yeast culture was as old as the bakery itself. You have to keep using the exact same culture and adding new ingredients if you want to make the bread always taste the same.

When I was little and went to Grandma's for a visit, sometimes Papa-La would walk me to his bakery and show me the special big brick stoves in the basement where they baked the breads. The stoves were built at the same time the bakery was built, and they were so long they stretched out underneath the sidewalk. Papa-La's stoves were nothing like the stoves bakeries use today.

They had to use huge, long wooden pallets, which were called "peels," to get the loaves in and out of the ovens without burning their hands, cause the temperature in the stoves got unbelievably high. The loaves were tremendous—maybe four feet long—cause they were mostly made for restaurants.

But Grandma would always cut some up in smaller chunks and give it to anyone who came to the house. Even the milkman and the newspaper boy.

When Papa-La sold his bakery and retired, he was very sad. Mom said he was going through a "period of adjustment." Once when they came to our house, I saw Papa-La sitting in the den holding his head in his hands and crying. Mom told me later he was upset cause he found out that the people who bought the bakery destroyed the old brick stoves and put in new ones.

For about a year after that, Papa-La wouldn't do anything that he always loved to do, like pruning trees around his house and taking pictures of flowers and birds. But then he started to get adjusted to being retired. And now he likes pruning trees and taking pictures again. He's working on a collection of nature photographs that he plans to make a book from.

Lots of people around New Jersey still remember Papa-La's famous rye bread. Like once when we went to Ridge Mountain Inn for Mother's Day with Grandma and Papa-La, the owner came over and recognized my grandfather, and they started talking about how bread isn't like it used to be in the old days when Papa-La was making it.

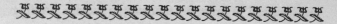

Five

At the end of school today Mr. Desnick came over to me while I was getting my books out of my locker and said he saw my name on the list of girls going on the bus to East Bradley on Saturday.

I got so nervous when he said it that I couldn't think of anything intelligent to say back. I blurted out something dumb about how tired I'd be cause my birthday party was going to be the night before, and then he said the ride was very long and I could always take a nap on someone's shoulder.

That really embarrassed me, cause I couldn't help imagining my head on Mr. Desnick's shoulder, even though I'm sure he didn't mean *him*. I know he saw me blushing, cause my face got hot right away when he said it. I hope he doesn't think I thought he meant *his* shoulder.

Then he said something really weird, which I'm not sure I understood exactly. He was looking at me in that steady way he looks at you, and he said, "You know, Stevie, you're the kind of girl who looks like you feel good when you run." I was kind of relieved when Jenny came by then and said our bus was waiting and if I didn't hurry I'd miss it.

Actually, I do feel good when I'm running, at least after the first few minutes when I start out feeling tired and out of breath. I wonder why, with all the running I do, I still feel out of breath at the beginning most of the time.

Anyway, what I like best is the part of the run that begins in the middle—when I'm not out of breath anymore and I get into a kind of rhythm. I begin to feel a hotness up and down the front of my thighs.

Mom doesn't like me to wear shorts when it's cold out. She says my legs will get all chapped. But unless it's really freezing, I like the way it feels running in shorts much better than warm-ups.

The other thing I like when I'm running is the way I feel in my head. I guess I daydream a lot when I'm running, cause I'm off by myself where no one can get to me. Sometimes I just think of things that've been going on with friends and school and stuff like that, and sometimes I make up stories that would be nice if they were true.

Lots of times lately I think about **Mr. Desnick** when I'm running. One story I like to imagine is what would happen if there was a huge snowstorm one day at the end of school, after all the busses were gone, and if I was the last person to come back from running cross-country.

Mr. Desnick would be in the field house when I come in, and we would be the only people left in the building. The snow would be so high by then that we couldn't leave the field house, and all the telephone lines would be down and the electricity would go out too at some point.

In the story we have to spend the whole night together talking in the field house. And because it gets very cold in the middle of the night—there's also no heat because of the snowstorm—we have to hold each other to keep warm. And then we start kissing, of course. Oh, I'd also have some Almond Joys in my locker so we could eat them instead of real food, cause there wouldn't be any, when we get hungry.

Daddy looked scary when I went in to kiss him good night. I only went because Mom told me I should. It's not like her to do that. We're not the kind of family they always show on TV, where everyone kisses their mother and father before going to sleep. We just say good night and go up to our rooms. Or if we're already in our room, we just go to bed when it's time. So it was a little strange when

Mom came in my room and made a point of telling me it would be nice to go kiss Daddy good night.

When I walked into their room, he was sitting up very straight in the chair on the other side of the bed by the window. It's the chair he usually uses just for hanging his jacket over the back and to sit on for putting shoes on. His eyes were closed when I walked in, but not the way eyes are closed when you're sleeping. They were closed like he was squeezing them closed.

I called out from the other side of the room, "Night, Daddy," as I came in. I guess I kind of wanted to give him notice, since the door was wide open and I didn't bother knocking. I felt like I shouldn't be seeing him without his knowing I was there. He said, "Hi, Babes," but not the way he usually sounds. His eyes were still clenched tight, and his voice sounded hoarse and faint.

As I got closer to his side of the room, I saw he was gripping the arms of his chair very tight, and the knuckles on his hands were all white. I looked at his face again, which was very red, and I thought he looked like he was in pain.

I feel like a coward for what I did then, but I couldn't make myself go any closer. I just said in a fake, gay voice, "See you in the morning, Daddy," and turned around and walked out. I don't think he answered, but I was rushing and might've missed it. I just couldn't bear the thought of kissing him while he looked that way.

Come to think of it, I can't ever remember

another time Daddy has just been *sitting* in that chair. It's such a straight, stiff-looking chair, and that's how Daddy looked sitting in it—straight and stiff. As though he couldn't get comfortable in that chair, or in the room, or anywhere at all. He also looked very far away.

Six

Jenny's mother picked us up after track practice today and dropped us off at Jamesway to shop for dress-up supplies for my slumber party. She was doing a big grocery shopping at the Acme, so we had practically an hour to browse around Jamesway and look for stuff.

It was really nice of Mrs. Pryor to do it, since it was for my party and should've been my mother who did the taking. But Mom had to take Dad out to the hospital for some tests, and Jenny's mother and Mom talked on the phone and made the arrangements.

I know what Jenny means when she says her mother really wants to do things for her. Mrs.

Pryor actually asked us if we wanted her to help us find what we needed at Jamesway. Jenny told her point blank we'd rather do it alone, which was a little rude the way she said it when her mother was just being nice to offer. Mom would never do that. She'd just tell us to be sure to finish up by a certain time so we wouldn't keep her waiting when she was ready to leave.

But I'm glad we were by ourselves at Jamesway, cause it wouldn't've been nearly as much fun if Mrs. Pryor came. First we found a wig for me—one of those very tightly curled ones with medium-length blond hair. My hair's brown and straightish and down to my shoulders, so I look completely different in the wig. I have to roll my own hair up in a barrette on top of my head to put the wig on so my hair won't show.

The wig looks a little like the speech teacher Miss Porter's hair. I know she's considered very sexy by the upper class girls at school, cause Jenny told me her sister Gwenn and her friends think she's gorgeous but that she flirts too much with the boys.

Gwenn told Jenny Miss Porter always wears her shirt unbuttoned one button too far, and when she leans over a certain way, which she always does around the boys' desks, you can see straight in. You must be able to see a lot, cause Gwenn's friend Mary Beth, who sits next to Steve Sugarman, who's the handsomest boy in the school, says Miss Porter wears the kind of bra that fastens in the front.

Then we got fake fingernails and some very dark red nail polish for me. Jenny got silver, which I think looks hideous, it's so unnatural. And we also got more eye makeup, even though we each have some. We wanted to have all new stuff for the party.

Since we still had lots of time before Mrs. Pryor was going to be back, we decided to check out the nightgowns and underwear. We saw this really perfect nightgown made out of some material you could see right through, like very thin, royal blue gauze, but it cost $12.99, and we didn't have enough money for that plus everything else we needed. Also, Jenny said the material looked too stiff and that it would probably give a rash.

I did buy something else, though. A size double-D-cup bra. The big, thick kind with bones and three hooks up the back that very busty women like the school nurse, Mrs. Scrib, wear. We're going to stuff it with tissue paper, and I'll wear it under Mom's black nightie. The only problem is that the bra straps, which are white, will show since the nightie has only very thin spaghetti-type straps that don't cover anything.

It'd be better at least for the bra to be black, but the one I bought was out on a shelf where you could just help yourself, and I was too embarrassed to ask a saleslady for another one.

When Mrs. Pryor dropped me off at home, it was around six o'clock. I noticed Mom's station wagon next to Daddy's car in the garage and remembered they had gone to the hospital together for Daddy's tests. Usually he doesn't get home 'til around seven, so I was surprised at first to see both cars in the garage until I remembered why.

My hands were full with bags from Jamesway, so I rang the bell. When no one answered, I let myself in the kitchen door, and when I dropped my knapsack on the floor as I came in, cause I couldn't manage everything, my kind, considerate brother Robby didn't even get off the stool he was sitting on to help me. "Thanks, pal," I said, and all he said back was, "For what?" He's so out of it.

Mom came in the kitchen and said, "Hi, Stephanie. Get what you needed?" I began to tell her what fun we'd had and how much good stuff for the party we got, when the timer started buzzing real loud the way it does.

Mom was already fixing salad at the sink by then, so she called over to Robby, who was right by the oven, to turn it off. He's so lazy it's disgusting. He said, "Geez, Mom, can't you see I'm reading?"

All he was doing was thumbing through an old *Sports Illustrated*. Mom grabbed a dish towel and went over to the oven to do it herself. I asked her if she was going to let my lazy blob of a brother get away with that, and all she said was, "Stephanie, you know I don't like name calling. Robby's angry with me because we've just had an argument about his Halloween costume."

"I don't notice when I've had an argument that *I* get excused from doing things!" I told her.

Then Robby muttered, "Shut up, Stevie. You're not my mother."

And I told him, cause it's true, "Thank God! That would be a fate worse than death."

Mom told us to be quiet or we'd both have to go to our rooms, but I was planning to go straight to mine anyway, which is what I did.

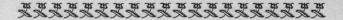

Seven

Later at dinner I had to live through a replay of the Halloween costume argument Mom had with Robby.

Mom and Dad don't allow toy guns and rifles and stuff like that, cause they say they've seen too much violence and don't believe in kids making believe they're murdering each other.

I can't see what toy guns have to do with real murder, but I don't care whether we're allowed to have them or not since I never wanted to play with guns anyway. But Robby has always wanted them and argues with Mom and Dad all the time about it.

The arguments are always the same, and it's really boring to have to sit through a whole replay of something I've heard a million times. It helps when I think about running, which is what I do sometimes when I'm really bored.

I pretend I'm on a trail in the woods somewhere and that I have to find a way to run around the trees and streams and rocks, which are all over the place. I kind of carve trails in my head. It's like tracing mazes in game books. I do this all the time in Miss Yamaguchi's English class, cause I can't stand listening to her.

It started with Robby saying he was going to be a marine for Halloween and needed a toy rifle for his costume. When Mom said he'd have to do without the rifle, he whined, "You can't be a marine without anything to defend yourself." Mom started telling her story for the umteenth time about when they announced that Kennedy was shot while she was a freshman at Barnard.

"My friends and I were sitting in the Annex having lunch, and suddenly everyone was shushing everyone, and the room went completely quiet. I even remember the radio—it was one of those big, old-fashioned pieces of furniture—not like the little radios you kids have today."

I was in my head running at the point Mom said this, and suddenly I imagined a big, old-fashioned radio like a huge boulder in the middle of the trail. I could hear Mom talking, but it felt like I was far away, and her voice was muffled by the sound of my feet falling on the ground as I ran.

"When they announced that President Kennedy was shot and on his way to the hospital," Mom was saying, "and that it wasn't certain whether he was dead or alive, half the girls in the room began to cry."

At that point Robby goes, "Aw, Mom, you always tell that stupid story. When you're in college you don't cry in front of other people." And Mom started in with how kids in her day believed in ideals and how they all campaigned for Kennedy and marched in Civil Rights demonstrations with Martin Luther King.

Then dumb Robby asked, "Is he the guy they give the day off from school for? They shot him too, didn't they?" I heard a gunshot in my head and saw a hunter with an orange hat hiding behind a tree, and then I saw a big, huge deer fall up ahead right across the trail. Just as I was about to hurdle the dead deer, Daddy launched into a whole elaborate explanation of the Civil Rights movement, which we'd all heard before.

Mom and Dad actually met on a march in Washington when they were in college, even though Mom was from Barnard in New York City and Daddy went to Dartmouth in New Hampshire. But a lot of people came from all over for the Civil Rights marches in those days.

You'd never know Mom and Dad did things like

that when they were younger. Now they're just like everyone else's parents and have nothing to do with politics except when they vote, which doesn't really count since everyone does it.

Mom finally interrupted Dad, who gets a little carried away at times like this, and updated her usual story with a comment about John Lennon and President Reagan and the Pope and how violent our whole society is.

Then she said in her voice which means End-of-Argument-and-the-Answer-Is-No, "And that's why your father and I simply cannot sanction the use of weapons, toy or otherwise, in our home."

"But I won't use the rifle in the house. I just need it for when we go trick or treating. Then you can give it away to the Salvation Army."

"I'm not about to pay good money for something so you can use it once and then give it away!" Mom was on the verge of screaming. I can always tell when she's getting close. Robby answered, "Then I'll buy it with my own money." I thought about the forty-nine dollar pair of Reebok running shoes I wanted, but I didn't have to ask to know the answer would be no.

By now they were off on another round, with Robby arguing that Mom wasn't being fair, cause she always says imagination is great and that we can make-believe anything we want. He also dragged in the business of how Officer Hayes's son Chip has a whole collection of toy howitzers and how *he* won the award for good student citizenship last year.

At one point Daddy winked at Robby and said he was talking just like a lawyer, and you could tell Daddy was actually proud of him, even though Robby was being a jerk.

Mom looked annoyed at Daddy for looking pleased with Robby and went into an explanation of the word "symbol," telling how toy guns are symbolic of real violence. It was really ridiculous, since Robby's way too dumb to understand anything that complicated. He even got a C minus in English last year, and that was because Mrs. Kazan never flunks anyone.

When Mom said "symbol," I saw a tree in a forest with outlines of hidden animals and things in it like the pictures in little kids' workbooks where you have to figure out where the objects are and then color them in.

Robby finally realized he wasn't getting a rifle no matter what he said, and he stood up and screamed at Mom, "You and your symbols can go to hell," and ran out of the room. A picture flashed across my mind of a kid scribbling wildly with a big red crayon all over the hidden objects page in his book.

Daddy pushed his chair away from the table and said in his I'll-Take-Charge voice, "Let me handle this, Joan." And *that* was dinnertime in the Farr family. Nothing like the Waltons on TV.

Eight

My birthday party was a real bomb. Nothing went the way it was supposed to. About an hour after everyone arrived, something horrible happened. I know I'll never forget it, and I swear I'll never give another party as long as I live.

We were all having pizza in the kitchen. Everyone but Rachel, cause she got the flu and had to cancel at the last minute.

Suddenly Mom came into the kitchen looking positively white in the face. She asked me to come inside, and I knew something horrible was about to happen. I got really scared when I saw the way she looked, and I can still taste the pizza I was eating, .cause I was having the feeling you get when you're about to throw up, and the taste of vomit got mixed with the taste of pizza in my mouth.

After that I couldn't eat another thing for the whole night. Not even my cake. The last taste I remember from my birthday dinner is pizza mixed with vomit. I don't know if I'll ever eat pizza again.

Mom kind of led me away from the kitchen and into the den, and then she told me we were having an emergency. Daddy was bleeding—she called it hemorrhaging—from the scar on his back where he was operated on last year, and an ambulance was coming to the house to get him. She was rushing very fast through all the explanations, cause Daddy was upstairs alone bleeding and needed her. She didn't say this was why she was rushing, but of course I knew why.

"Now listen, Stephanie. I called Jenny's mom, and she's coming right over to spend the night with you and your friends while I'm at the hospital. So you can have your party anyway." Everything was happening so fast, and I was so confused by now I was almost crying, and I told Mom I didn't want a party anymore.

"Come on now, Stephanie. You have a houseful of guests, and it's your job to take care of them. I'll call the house as soon as I can from the hospital and let you know how Daddy is."

As Mom was saying this last part, she was just about out of the room already. Her voice had changed from her Worried-Mother voice to her impatient, Time's-Up-Now voice. She obviously had to get back to Daddy really quickly.

Something told me I'd better not tell her again that I didn't want a party anymore, even though I wanted everyone in the kitchen to just disappear so I wouldn't have to face them.

Later I saw the bloody sheets Mrs. Pryor was taking out of their room on her way to the washer in the basement. It was unbelievable how much blood was on them. I'm glad I kept my mouth shut about not wanting my party anymore. Maybe Daddy almost bled to death up there. I bet every second counted.

I never did get to see Daddy really before they took him away. Except at the very end when the men from the ambulance were carrying him out on a stretcher. But then he was all wrapped up so tight in bandages or sheets or something that he didn't look bloody anymore.

His eyes were closed like he was sleeping, and I thought he looked like a mummy. Except with mummies they wrap the faces, and I know they didn't wrap Daddy's face cause I remember his eyes being closed and thinking he looked dead. But I knew he couldn't be dead or they wouldn't be rushing anymore. Thank God none of my friends saw anything! Or at least if they did, thank God no one said anything.

After Mom told me what was happening, I went back into the kitchen, and I guess my automatic self took over, cause without having to make myself do it I was telling my friends in a calm, cool, collected voice that my father was going to the hospital because he was sick—I didn't mention the part about the hemorrhaging—and that we could keep having our party anyway and that Jenny's mother was coming over soon to stay with us.

It was all so unreal the way it happened. My taking charge like that when I was so scared I didn't know what I was doing. I've always heard that when you're in shock, you sometimes act the way you're supposed to without feeling the feelings that go with what you're doing. Something inside me kept thinking that Mom would be proud of me for acting this way even though I must've been in shock.

The automatic feeling never really went away that night. It was a little like when I'm pretending to be there in class but I'm really off running in my head somewhere else. Except the night of my party the inside feelings weren't about good things, like running.

I went through all the motions of my birthday party—dressing up with the girls, putting makeup on, wearing the blond, curly wig from Jamesway and the long red fingernails, even taking pictures with Daddy's Polaroid—but inside I felt sad and far away.

I remember thinking how strange it was that I asked Daddy to teach me how to use the camera cause we'd be too embarrassed if he took pictures of us dressed up that way. He wouldn't've been able to take pictures of us after all.

I guess some things are just meant to be a certain way, and maybe my learning to use the camera means Daddy wasn't meant to be at my party.

In the middle of taking a picture of Sammy (that's what we call Samantha), who was wearing a skin-tight pink leotard stuffed with two of Mom's tennis balls and pretending to be Cheryl Tiegs as the Playboy Centerfold, I remembered what Daddy said when he was showing me how to use the camera. It made me want to cry when I remembered it. It was the only time all night, until everyone else was sleeping, that I didn't have that feeling of being an automatic person.

A couple of nights before my party, Daddy and I were practicing taking Polaroid pictures of our dog Biscuit. We named Biscuit Biscuit because he's tan like the color of a dog biscuit. But whenever we tell people about him, it always comes out sounding funny, cause we wind up saying something like, "You know, when our dog Biscuit was a puppy . . ." and people think we're talking about a dog biscuit instead of a dog. It's impossible to explain this in words unless you read it.

Anyway, we were taking pictures of Biscuit the dog (that's how we get around confusing people about his name), and finally I got a really good one of Daddy down on the floor on his hands and knees with his tongue hanging out pretending he was a dog, and Biscuit sitting next to him watching Daddy with his head cocked and one scraggly ear hanging down.

The way the picture came out it looked so cute because Biscuit practically had the expression of a person. You could imagine him thinking how silly Daddy looked pretending he was a dog. Daddy and I got hysterical looking at that picture after it was developed.

I played a joke on Daddy by running away with the print and telling him I was sending a copy to his boss, Mr. Frye, for Christmas. Daddy took off after me to get it back, and Biscuit started running after me too. It was all so funny.

When we finally stopped laughing and Daddy got up off the floor like a grown-up human being again, I hugged him and said, "Thanks for teaching me to use your camera, Daddy. I guess since you were so nice, I won't really send a copy to Mr. Frye!" And we laughed again.

Then Daddy said, in a much more serious voice than normal, "You know, Stevie, there are lots of things you're getting ready to do for yourself." He put his hand under my chin and kind of squeezed it the way he does and said, "That's the meaning of growing up, Stevie. Some day we no longer need our parents to do things for us or even to show us how anymore."

It sounded really sad the way he said it, but I

never thought about it 'til just then when he was gone and I was taking a picture of Sammy. It made me want to cry, but I couldn't let myself because my party was going on, and I had to keep acting as if everything was OK.

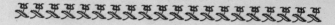

Nine

Some time after two A.M. everyone fell asleep. Mrs. Pryor came upstairs around one and told us it was time to get out of our costumes and wash up for bed. She even helped us take off makeup with some cotton puffs and cold cream from a big jar Mom keeps in her medicine chest.

Sammy, Alyn, and Margo slept on the floor in my bedroom, and Jenny and Carol slept in my bed. I slept on the floor, since I didn't think the hostess should take the bed. Even though it was very late, I didn't feel tired at all.

Earlier in the party Mom called and told me things with Daddy were pretty much under control, but I could tell from her voice, which didn't sound very under control, that things were pretty bad. She sounded like she'd been crying or else that she suddenly had a really bad cold, which wasn't too likely since she didn't have one before she left.

After everyone was sleeping, I tried for a while to fall asleep but just couldn't, so I finally got up and tiptoed downstairs. I wasn't hungry, but I went to the refrigerator anyway and opened it up like I do when I am hungry and I'm looking for an idea for what I feel like eating. But the minute I smelled the smell of food, I felt like vomiting again, so I slammed the door shut real hard and then got worried I'd wake one of the girls or Mrs. Pryor, and I really didn't want to have to be with anyone then.

I walked through the kitchen and into the den, and when I looked in the den the scariest thing happened. I saw something move and then realized it was someone all curled up and pretending to be sleeping under the plaid blanket we keep on the sofa in there. I thought it was a stranger who got into the house and was trying to hide. I knew the person wasn't sleeping, cause when I came near and looked in the den he moved real quickly to cover himself so I wouldn't see him.

Then I realized it was Robby, and I couldn't believe it when I saw he was home and must've been in the house the whole night—all through my party and Daddy's emergency and everything—and I never thought of him once the entire time. It made me feel awful, cause I remembered arguing with

Mom that I wanted him out of the house for my birthday. And when it came down to it, I never knew he was here anyway.

I had just gotten so scared and when I saw it was Robby I was so relieved that I actually felt angry. It was strange to be angry when I was really relieved, and it reminded me of something Mom once told me about how she felt the time I got lost in Bamberger's when I was little and she and all the sales ladies were frantically looking everywhere for me because they were scared I'd fall down the escalator.

When Mom finally found me I was playing in a dress rack, and even though she was really relieved, she said she spanked me very hard until I cried and then hugged me right away afterward, cause she didn't know if she was angry I got lost or glad I got found.

"Robby," I nearly screamed at him, because I was still kind of shaky from being scared. "What are you doing and where have you been all night?" He buried himself entirely under the blanket so I couldn't see his head or feet or any part of him.

"Robby, come on out now. It's almost morning. Have you been there all night? Didn't Mrs. Pryor make you go to bed?"

"Fuck Mrs. Pryor," came from under the blanket.

"Robby, cut it out! And get out from under the blanket. You're acting like an idiot."

"Shut up, Stevie. I hate you. Go away." Suddenly the blanket started heaving up and down, and Robby was making really weird, hyena-sounding wails as though he was pretending he was a wild animal. Until I realized he wasn't pretending. He was crying—sobbing really—very hard, and the blanket was moving up and down, cause Robby was shaking from crying so hard.

I always tell people I hate my brother, and I really think I usually do, but when I saw him there crying under the blanket, I think I realized I must really love Robby a lot underneath it all.

I can almost never remember feeling sorry for Robby the way I did that night, cause usually he's in some kind of trouble he makes for himself. Like not getting homework done and then lying to teachers that he did it and left it home. I guess I knew he didn't make his own trouble this time, and maybe that's why I felt so sorry for him.

I went over to the sofa and was going to sit down next to him, the way Daddy sits by me sometimes when I'm in bed and we're talking. But with Robby all bunched up under the blanket and shaking so hard, I really couldn't find a place to sit. So I sat down on the floor right next to the sofa and put my hand on the blanket to let him know I was there. I think it was his hunched-up back I was patting, or rubbing.

I didn't really know what to do, but I thought I shouldn't try to talk right away. I was feeling very grown-up, as though I was the mother and had to take care of a hurt child.

53

It seemed like I sat there rubbing Robby's back under that blanket for a real long time, until Robby finally pulled his head out a little and stopped crying and heaving up and down. His face was very red and hot-looking and all wet from crying. Little fuzzy, woolly bits from the blanket were pressed against his face, which made it look dirty.

He let out a big sigh and sort of collapsed down flat on his tummy on the sofa, and then he did a really un-Robby kind of thing. He took his hand out from under the blanket and reached over to my face and pulled me close like he was going to kiss my cheek or hug me, and then instead of giving me a kiss, which I expected, he whispered in my ear, "I'm so scared, Stevie. Do you think Daddy's dead from bleeding?"

I told him no and asked him if he got to speak with Mom when she called. Since Mrs. Pryor spoke to Mom first and then came in to get me, I figured she gave Robby a chance to talk with Mom before or after I did.

"Mom never called," Robby said. I told him she did call, cause I spoke to her and Daddy was better.

"She did not call. I never heard her call." Robby was beginning to get angry again.

"Where were you all night anyway, Robby? I never realized you were here all during the time my party was going on."

"I told Mom I was sleeping at Billy Barnett's house, 'cause I knew you didn't want me here."

"But when did you come home?" I asked him.

"I never came home because I never left. I was hiding in the crawl space by the back stairs to Mom and Dad's room, and they didn't know I was there, but I saw everything through the cracks in the door when Daddy got hurt and was bleeding, and I heard Mom call the ambulance and everything. It was a horrible bloody mess. You wouldn't believe how much Daddy bled. I know he's dead by now. You can't live if you lose that much blood."

"Oh, Robby, how awful. How could you stand being in there all night?" Now *I* felt like crying.

"I wasn't in there all night. When the ambulance came and everyone left, I went into my room and shut the door. 'Til stupid Mrs. Pryor walked in without knocking around eleven. She said she saw a light under the door and wanted to turn it off, cause she thought I was sleeping away and no one was in my room. She tried to talk to me about what happened, but I didn't want to talk to dumb Jenny's mother."

"Listen, Robby. Mom *did* call. You must've not heard the phone 'cause you were in your room with the door closed."

I didn't know if I should tell Robby Daddy was OK, cause I really didn't think he could be too good from the sound of Mom's voice. But I knew Robby thought Daddy must be dead, and I wanted to make him feel better, so I said, "And Daddy's all right. The bleeding is under control. Everything is going to be OK." Even though I didn't believe what I was saying was true.

Then Robby went absolutely wild and started screaming, and it was a miracle he didn't wake the others up. "You're lying, Stevie, just like Mom lied. Daddy's dead. They took him away and he was bleeding to death. I saw him. You didn't see 'cause you were eating pizza and playing movie stars. He's dead, and he's never coming back. And Mom's a liar and always has been, and you're a liar too." And the shaking and sobbing started all over.

Usually when Robby gets in one of his rages, I really hate him and want to hit him or scream something really mean at him. But maybe because Mom wasn't there, and I was feeling kind of like a parent, I just sat on the floor and didn't move or scream back or leave the room or anything while Robby was hollering.

When he finally stopped screaming I got up and made a place to sit by him on the sofa. I think I was half sitting on the top of one of his legs, cause he was still under the blanket taking up practically the whole space.

I rubbed his back some more, and his crying and shaking calmed down, and just before he fell asleep in a big, exhausted heap, he turned his head toward me with one cheek lying flat on the sofa and the other cheek all fuzzied with wool bits of blanket and said, "I don't really hate you, Stevie." And for what I think was the first time I ever said this in my life, I told him, "I love you, Robby." And then he was asleep.

Ten

Grandma and Papa-La were here when we woke up this morning. Grandma said Mom called her at six thirty this morning from the hospital to let her know Daddy went in again.

When we woke up, Mrs. Pryor and Grandma were already making pancakes and sausages, so we all went into the kitchen and sat around the breakfast table in robes and nighties.

Grandma had the table set the way she does when she takes care of us when Mom and Dad are away. She always puts out coffee cups and saucers like grown-ups use, but instead of coffee she fills them with juice or milk or whatever we're having to drink for that meal.

My friends really liked the cups and saucers, and they all started imitating fancy ladies drinking tea. Only we were drinking fresh-squeezed orange juice.

That's something else Grandma always does. She says the stuff that comes frozen in cans has nothing left to it, and the only way to get what she calls "God's goodness" from oranges is to squeeze them fresh. Mom says it's nice of Grandma to bother, but that it takes too much time for her (meaning Mom) to do it every day.

Robby seemed pretty embarrassed to be with so many girls, so he took his plate and went in the den to watch cartoons while he ate. I felt kind of sorry for him looking so self-conscious and left out. And I felt guilty again about making such a big deal before my party about his being away from the house so he wouldn't bother us. No one ever really saw him the whole time, or if they did, they couldn't've minded him being there, cause he didn't say a word or do anything.

After a while Grandma told Papa-La to stop flirting with all the girls and to go keep Robby company inside. I was glad when she said that, so Robby wouldn't be all alone in the den.

Carol said she thought my grandfather was really young-looking and handsome. I always feel proud when people say that. Grandma liked it too, and she told everyone how Papa-La kept young walking the five miles back and forth between their house and his bakery in Trenton for forty-three years "rain or shine, sleet or snow." She always says that when people say how young Papa-La looks.

After breakfast I tried on my birthday present—a pair of Reebok racing flats. All the girls at my party chipped in so they could buy them for me. Everyone must've given at least eight dollars, cause the "Aztek Princess"—that's the name of the shoe —costs almost fifty dollars. It was really neat of them to do this for me.

The note they put on the box was a big foot someone drew and cut out of cardboard. It said, "Happy Birthday to our friend Stevie. Good luck at East Bradley." And everyone signed on a separate toe in all different colored inks. Even Rachel who wasn't there cause she had the flu.

The running shoes fit perfectly and looked great. They're mostly bright blue with swooshes of red and yellow on the sides. Real sharp-looking, but not too flashy. And they have these little plastic loops to thread the laces through, instead of the usual holes.

I put them on over a pair of old knee socks that were lying out on the dryer, with my nightie and robe still on, and ran around the kitchen and living room a few times, kind of exaggerating my stride to make it look funny. Everyone was hysterical when I bounced around the breakfast table and leaped across the floor like a clumsy ballerina. Grandma told me to watch the coffeepot so I wouldn't get burned, but she was laughing so hard she had to wipe tears from her eyes.

It was about the most fun part of my whole party

for me. It made me almost forget the night before. But right in the middle of it the phone rang, and I heard Papa-La answer it in the den. I could tell right away it was Mom calling from the hospital. After a while Papa-La hung up and came in the kitchen. I could see by his face the news wasn't too good. He didn't say anything out loud, but he gave Grandma a look that suddenly changed her whole mood. She started cleaning up real fast then, and Mrs. Pryor told the girls it was time to get dressed so she could drive them home.

When the girls were all dressed and packed up, everyone climbed into Jenny's station wagon and sang happy birthday to me as they pulled out of the driveway. Jenny opened the sunroof and stuck a hand up with a V-for-Victory sign. I felt kind of let down as they were leaving, cause there was nothing good left to look forward to.

As soon as they were all gone, Papa-La told us Mom called to say Daddy was OK, but they had to operate last night and we wouldn't be able to visit for a while 'til Daddy was rested. Grandma asked, "How's Joan?" Joan is Mom's name, and Grandma is Mom's mother. Grandma sounded very worried about her. Papa-La said she was fine but tired and was coming home later in the afternoon to see us and to shower and change.

Maybe it was the lack of sleep from the night before, but suddenly I just felt exhausted. I was thinking of going out for a run in my new running shoes, but I felt like I wouldn't make it around the block. Instead I told Grandma I was going up to straighten my room and maybe get some rest. I asked her to wake me by ten thirty so I could get to the high school in time to catch the bus to East Bradley for the boys' meet.

When I got up to my room I saw on my clock it was only nine, but I felt really tired and worn out, as though a whole day had gone by already. I lay down on my bed and thought about my party and how much I wanted last night to come and how I really didn't have any fun after all. It made me feel angry at Daddy for getting so sick in the middle of it and ruining the mood. It just didn't feel party-ish anymore, once Mom and Dad left for the hospital, and there was no use pretending, cause it didn't help.

I tried to cheer myself up thinking about my new track shoes and the girls all singing me happy birthday as they were driving away, but I kept remembering the sound of the siren getting fainter and fainter as the ambulance was taking Daddy away last night.

And then I fell asleep and slept for about an hour, when I woke up to the sound of the telephone ringing. It was Jenny calling to see how Daddy was. Right after I hung up with her, Rachel called to say she heard from Sammy about Daddy and how was he. Then Grandma mentioned that while I was napping, Mrs. Lehman, who plays in Mom's tennis group, called to ask how we were and if she could do anything to help out. She said she heard about Daddy from Margo Cotton's mom. They live next door to each other. I wonder how many other people know by now. You'd think we were war orphans the way people are acting!

It made me feel funny when Jenny and Rachel called, cause I really didn't feel like talking about Daddy getting sick and going to the hospital. If it hadn't been for my party and their being here, no one would know what happened anyway. It's really no one's business but ours.

Then I got dressed in warm-ups and my new Reeboks, grabbed a yogurt and a plastic spoon on the way out the door, and Papa-La drove me to the high school, cause if I'd walked I might've missed the bus with the boys' team, which was leaving at eleven thirty for East Bradley.

When Papa-La dropped me off, he said to make sure to call him when the bus got back so he could come and get me. I told him I could just run home, since I was dressed for it and didn't have anything to carry, but he said he didn't like the idea of my coming home alone late in the afternoon when it might be getting dark. I told him I do it every day after school, but he said to be sure to call anyway, cause he would feel better if I did. Papa-La is so old-fashioned. But to make him feel better, I told him I'd call.

Eleven

Jenny's sister Gwenn sure knew what she was talking about! Mr. Desnick certainly is a lech, even though I was way too naive to read the writing on the wall.

It was kind of weird what happened today, cause after all the thinking I've been doing about Mr. Desnick, when my big moment with him came, it wasn't what I wanted at all, and I was scared to death. At first I thought it might be cause of what happened last night with Daddy and my still being upset and all, but now I think no matter what happened I wouldn't've liked what Mr. Desnick was doing.

He saved a seat for me on the bus going to East

Bradley this morning. As soon as he saw me coming down the aisle between the two rows of seats, he sort of grabbed my arm and pulled me across him to the seat by the window. Then he said, with his face practically *in* my face, "Hey kiddo, now that you're fourteen, how do you feel?" I don't think it was my imagination that he looked at my chest when he said it.

I was really tired from last night, so when the bus started up I leaned my head away from him and against the window, but I didn't sleep the whole ride, cause I could feel his leg rubbing up against mine. It wasn't real obvious the way he was doing it, but I kept moving my leg away, and every time the bus lurched a little bit, he would put his leg back where it'd touch mine.

At one point he ran his hand over his thigh like he was scratching it, but our legs were so close together he was really touching my leg at the same time.

Even though it wasn't the same, I kept feeling like I did the time I was in New York City visiting Aunt Martha, and I rode the bus up Madison Avenue to her apartment by myself while Mom went to meet Dad for lunch. I took a seat toward the back of the bus, and the only other person near me was a revolting old man sitting right across from me.

He wasn't actually sitting there when I got on the bus, but during the ride he got up and moved to the seat across from me. When I looked at him at one point, I saw he was holding his thing out of his fly and sticking it straight out at me and kind of wobbling it around in the air. He was smiling a kind of idiot grin at me the whole time.

It was definitely the most disgusting thing I've ever seen. But I was so scared and shocked I couldn't move. I just sat there, trying to look like I didn't notice what he was doing and praying that he wouldn't follow me off the bus, until we got to Aunt Martha's stop at 84th Street. I waited 'til the very last minute before the doors were going to close again, and then I bolted out onto the street so he wouldn't have time to get off too.

When I told Jenny about what happened on the bus in New York, she told me the same thing happened to her sister's friend Mary Beth, who's very experienced and knows a lot about sex. She just reported the man who was doing it to the bus driver, who went back and kicked the guy off the bus.

Jenny said Gwenn told her men like that aren't usually rapists. She said they were perverts and that they had to be sick to do those things. I don't think I'd ever have the nerve to do what Mary Beth did.

I guess I must not have really wanted what I thought I did when I imagined what it would be like to be close with Mr. Desnick. The scenes I made up about him in my head all happened so differently. Sometimes I would imagine us just holding hands and walking together. Or maybe he would kiss me after a while. But mostly we would talk together, and he would ask me lots of questions about myself, or tell me stories about when he was a young kid in high school, like me.

I always imagined feeling kind of warm and safe when we were together. But what happened today was nothing like that at all. I kept wanting to get away from him and feeling like what he was doing was disgusting. I didn't like any of it at all.

I was also very nervous and embarrassed that someone might notice. Dick Miller was sitting behind us and having a conversation with Mickey Brady on the other side of the aisle and two seats forward. So every time he wanted to say something, Dick would stand up and kind of hold onto the back of my seat, so he could call across the bus to Mickey. And whenever he did that, I was sure he saw Mr. Desnick's leg right up against mine. I was pretending to be sleeping the whole time, cause I didn't know what else to do.

Maybe what happened means I'm not going to like sex in real life and that I'm going to be frigid when I grow up.

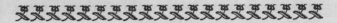

Twelve

When we got to East Bradley, some of the runners who already knew the course came over to meet us and show us where we'd be running. You never saw anything as beautiful as those woods behind that school. Streams and rocks and places where the trees are so thick it feels like a forest.

There was a light snowfall the other night, and you could actually see thousands and thousands of deer footprints in the snow that was still left on the sides of the path.

There were places where the trail was completely roofed over with the tangly limbs of trees all grown together like a canopy covering the trail. And then suddenly you'd run into a patch of sunlight where the trail was open to the sky.

I guess I was too busy looking at the scenery, or maybe it happened cause I was so exhausted from the night before, but a couple of miles into the course I stumbled on an exposed tree root and went flying forward and landed on my hands and knees in the brambles on the side of the trail. I even bruised my face when my head landed, and both my legs got all cut up from the underbrush where I fell.

At first I was so stunned I just lay there, but then I began to feel the pain in my left ankle. When I looked down at it, it was already starting to swell, so I tried to sit up to untie my running shoe. But when I sat up I must've turned my ankle some more, cause it hurt so much I started to cry.

There I was all by myself on the side of the trail, crying and getting the chills, cause now that I wasn't moving and was only wearing shorts and a sweatshirt, my body was beginning to feel the cold.

A couple of upper class boys came by pretty soon after I fell, and when they saw me crying and holding my leg they came over to help. Jeb Gray told John Clugston to go get Desnick while he stayed with me, which was pretty nice of him. Especially since Jeb's in eleventh grade, and juniors practically never talk to freshmen.

"You're Stevie Farr, aren't you?" Jeb asked me. I couldn't believe he knew my name. When I told him that's who I was, he said, "I hear you run the 3.2 in nineteen. That's a pretty damn good time."

I was so amazed he knew my time that I forgot how much my ankle was hurting and started to change my position. But as soon as I moved, the pain was tremendous again, and I think I screamed, "Ow, it hurts," before I started crying again. I was so embarrassed to be crying in front of Jeb Gray that I wanted to die.

Next I knew he had actually taken off the shirt he had on under his sweatshirt and was offering it to me to wipe my face. When I looked up at him he was putting his sweatshirt back over his bare chest, and his hair was all mussed from taking the T-shirt and the sweatshirt off. He really looked gorgeous. I thought of Jenny and wanted to be home already so I could call her and tell her all about it.

"Think you'll be able to run on that ankle again this season?" Jeb was asking me. It was the first time, since I fell, that I thought about whether I'd be all right for running or not.

"I'll have to be better by the fourteenth. I'm running this course for the girls' conference, and they need me to win if we're going to take the meet."

"Well," Jeb said with the most adorable smile you've ever seen, "we'll just have to see what we can do to help you get better in time." And then he stooped down, put his arm under mine, reached way down around my waist with his hand, and told me to stand up.

I didn't feel like I was going to be able to make it up, but Jeb was holding me very tight and kind of pulling me up at the same time. I couldn't believe how strong he was.

"Don't put any weight on that foot, Stevie. Just see if you can hop a little ways like this."

I had to put my hand up on Jeb's shoulder to balance myself, and I felt kind of self-conscious about what we were doing. I had to keep telling myself this was a medical emergency and that it had nothing to do with sex or romance. But it still felt strange hobbling along with Jeb Gray's arm around my waist and my hand on his shoulder.

Thank God it wasn't Mr. Desnick who came back with John. Instead, John drove up in a jeep with the assistant coach of the East Bradley boys' track team, who took me over to the school infirmary. Everything happened so fast once the jeep got there that I didn't remember to thank Jeb for helping me. But before he ran off with John, he gave me a big smile and said, "See you, Stevie. Hope your ankle's OK."

All the way to the infirmary I was picturing Jeb's bare chest and his mussy hair, and I could still feel his arm around my waist where he was holding me before. I don't think I'm really going to be frigid when I'm older.

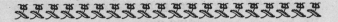

Thirteen

On the bus home I reread the instructions the nurse who took care of my ankle at East Bradley gave me. The intructions were printed on a green sheet of paper which said I should apply cold compresses for the first twenty-four hours and then soak my ankle in warm water after that. Whenever I can in between, I'm supposed to keep my leg with the sore ankle raised up. The nurse explained this is to keep the blood in my leg from going into the sore ankle and making it swell more.

She also gave me an ice pack to take with me on the bus ride home, and by the time the ride was over—I kept the ice on almost the whole time—my ankle was practically back to normal. I'm going to

71

do everything they say on the instruction sheet so I'll be able to train for the girls' meet on the fourteenth.

I sat with Lizzy Sneider on the trip home. She's a sophomore and a pretty nice person, even though she's very shy. Mom says she thinks Lizzy's shy cause her mother's that way. They go to the same dinner parties, and I've heard Mom say that Mrs. Sneider has trouble making conversation she's so shy.

Lizzy's the same way. When you're with her you have to be the one to start every topic, and then she'll just say something short in a slow, shy kind of way, like she wishes she didn't have to say anything at all. It can get pretty boring after a while, and pretty tiring too. But I wanted to be sure I was sitting with someone before Mr. Desnick got on the bus.

When he did get on the bus, I saw him look around and find a seat next to Gabriella Morehouse. She's a junior and not very popular with the boys or the girls. In fact, I can't think of anyone she really hangs around with. Mostly you see Gabriella sitting on the stairs around school and eating apples and reading by herself. The boys call her Gabriella Whorehouse behind her back.

I wonder if Mr. Desnick tried anything with her. And I wonder how she acted if he did. I kept looking at them and trying to figure out if anything was going on, but I couldn't really tell cause they were sitting toward the front of the bus, and Lizzy and I were pretty far back.

Jeb Gray was already sitting with John Clugston when I got on the bus, and I was so embarrassed when I had to hobble past him to get to where Lizzy was sitting. But when I went by he said in a nice, friendly voice, like we knew each other real well, "Hi, Stevie, how's the ankle?"

It wasn't what he said that made me blush, but I guess it was just the idea that Jeb Gray was calling me by my name in front of all those kids on the bus. I guess if you're as popular and self-confident as Jeb Gray, you can afford to have other kids see you talking to lower classmen.

I mumbled something about my ankle being better and congratulated him on his cross-country race. The team from Greensboro took first, third, and fifth places, and they won the meet. But Jeb took second for us. He looked pleased when I congratulated him.

When I got back to school, Mrs. Sneider was there waiting in the parking lot for Lizzy and offered to give me a lift home, so I didn't have to call Papa-La to come get me.

I don't know why I thought she'd know, but all I could think about on the drive to my house was that Mrs. Sneider was going to say she'd heard about Daddy going to the hospital. I was so relieved when she didn't say anything. Maybe she did know but was too shy to say it.

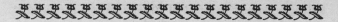

Fourteen

When I got home, Mom was back from the hospital. She looked terrible when I walked in and saw her sitting in the kitchen having tea with Grandma. She looked like she hadn't slept for a week. Big black circles under her eyes and no makeup and her hair kind of loose and frazzled.

She looked older too. When I compared her to Grandma, who's always kind of pink and plump-looking, Mom seemed small and worn out—like she was an old lady and Grandma was younger than she was. It made me think of those stupid television commercials where the mother and the daughter compare dishpan hands, and you see how the mother's hands look younger than the daughter's. It was weird seeing Mom like that. She usually looks pretty and perked-up.

The first thing Mom said when I came in was how sorry she was about my party last night. It surprised me when she said that, cause at my party she acted like everything would be just the same, even though we were having an emergency. I guess you have to put on that kind of an act in an emergency.

Then she said she had something special for me upstairs. We went up to her bedroom, and Mom went over to the dresser where there was a box wrapped up in pretty, shiny, tan paper with a big orange bow.

"This is a special gift Daddy got for you, Stephanie. He wanted to give it to you himself, but with what happened last night, that just wasn't possible. He asked me to give it to you now—for him."

I sat on Mom's bed and began to unwrap the box. I was opening it very slowly, cause for some reason I was kind of dreading seeing what was in it. I can't explain why I was feeling like I didn't want to know, but I just didn't feel the excited way I usually do when I'm opening up a present. I also wanted to make the moment last, as if once it was gone I would miss something that I couldn't get back again. Like something was ending or going away.

When I got the orange ribbon off, I carefully peeled off the scotch tape so I wouldn't rip the tan wrapping paper. Then I took the paper off and folded it in a big square and then a smaller square before I opened the box.

On top of the green tissue paper inside was a card which said, "For Stevie," on the envelope. It was written in Daddy's writing, which is the same kind of block print like kids use, which always looks so funny coming from a grown-up man.

The card in the envelope said, "Happy birthday all the years of your life. With miles of measureless love. Daddy."

I didn't put the card down with the paper and the ribbon. I just kept it in my hand while I finished unwrapping the present.

When I opened the tissue paper, I saw the face of a pedometer—the kind you attach to your waist and it hangs down your leg to clock miles when you run—staring up at me.

Then I looked at Mom and asked, "How is Daddy?" I saw her mouth twitch and her eyes fill with tears.

"Daddy's been through surgery, Stephanie. He's very weak and tired right now. It will take a while for him to regain his strength."

"Will Daddy be all right, Mom?" The wait until Mom answered was endless. I'm not sure I meant to ask like that. The words just kind of came out of me.

"I don't want to make any false promises, Stephanie. Daddy's very sick. He had a growth removed from his back last year, as you know, and we were hoping with the treatments there would be no more growths, but that's not what has happened, and . . ."

Something about the way Mom was talking made it suddenly click for me, and I could feel myself getting more furious than I can ever remember feeling before.

Suddenly a whole bunch of stuff came together in my head. It was like a kind of brain crash, if you know what I mean. I remembered Dr. Wechsler, the surgeon's, call a few months ago and how strange it seemed for him to be calling when Mom said Daddy just had the flu. I remembered all the trips to the hospital all through the last year since Daddy's operation. So many check-ups when Daddy was supposedly all better? Even at the time it'd seemed strange. And now it all seemed suddenly perfectly clear.

"You mean Daddy had a tumor and he has cancer, don't you? And you never even told me. Those were cancer treatments he was getting when you said he was having tests and check-ups all the time. Why did you lie to me?"

I was crying and practically screaming by now. I could hardly believe the way I sounded. I said some things I didn't even realize I ever thought or felt.

"Stephanie! How dare you call me a liar. We never lied to you. We tried to protect you from the pain and uncertainty of your father's condition. We didn't want to upset you—"

"Upset me?" Now I really let go and went wild. I

was crying so hard I couldn't see and screaming so loud I couldn't hear. "How can you expect me not to be upset with my own father dying of cancer and no one telling me what's going on. I'm not a baby anymore, even though you think I am. And anyway, I don't want any stupid pedometer to clock miles with. I want Daddy to help me, not some dumb gadget!"

And then I took the pedometer from the tissue paper it was lying in and heaved it as hard as I could against the wall. It struck Mom's dresser— Mom's antique dresser, which came from Grandma and Papa-La—and left a huge gash near the corner of the bottom drawer.

I ran across the room and stomped on the face of the pedometer 'til it was all smashed in. And then, with Mom shrieking, "Stephanie, stop it!" over and over again, I ran out—sore ankle and all—and into my room.

I slammed the door and threw myself on my bed, sobbing. And for the first time in my life, I knew what a person really feels like when they wish they were dead.

I must've fallen asleep after that, cause when I woke up I found Daddy's card all balled up in my hand. The big, block letters of his writing were smeared and blurry, and when I tried to smoothe the wrinkles out of the card and couldn't, I started crying all over again.

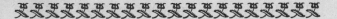

Fifteen

Grandma and Papa-La have been living with us since almost two weeks ago when they came the morning after my party. Mom's hardly been around since Daddy's been in the hospital. The last few nights she's even been sleeping in the hospital and only coming home to see us for a little while after school. Then she goes back to be with Daddy.

Last Sunday Robby and I went with Grandma and Papa-La to visit Daddy. Mom was already there when we came. It was a very quick visit, cause Daddy takes lots of medicine and sleeps most of the time.

He has a tube called an intravenous hooked into his arm and connected to a bottle with something that looks like water but is really some kind of liquid nourishment. The tube is stuck right into Daddy's vein, but when Robby asked him if it hurt, Daddy said he couldn't even feel it.

He was very pale—I guess from being inside for so long. And he looks very thin. The dripping liquid probably doesn't have nearly the calories of real food, which Daddy can't eat now.

Seeing Daddy that way made me want to get away from there as fast as I could. I was glad when the nurse came in and said it was time to say goodbye.

Before leaving I went over and gave Daddy a quick kiss on the forehead, and he squeezed my hand very weakly. I was nervous about bumping into the tube in his arm and worried that if something came loose it might be dangerous for him in his condition.

Daddy smiled when I kissed him, and I noticed how his lips were all dry and cracked-looking. I was glad he didn't ask anything about the pedometer. I hope he doesn't know.

In the car on the way home from the hospital, Grandma started crying. Papa-La kept saying, "Come, come, Mother. Come, come." He always calls Grandma "Mother."

When Jenny and I were walking to school today, she told me she thinks I'm crazy to be training as hard as I am for the East Bradley meet. She said she thinks I'm acting like running is the most important thing in the world. I think she's jealous cause I'm on the varsity and she's not.

"All you ever do anymore is run, run, run all the time, Stevie. You don't even have any time anymore for your friends."

"That's not true, Jen," I told her. "It's just that I have to be ready for the meet. The team's counting on me to win, and so is Mrs. Mackley."

"Geez, Stevie, you'd think you're the only one who matters on the whole team. It's not just you who's going to make us win or lose on Saturday. The other girls count too, you know."

"Yaa, but they need me to take first. They're expecting me too, and I don't want to let them down."

"Well," Jenny said, "I think you should know how the way you've been acting makes your friends feel. Rachel and Sammy were saying on Sunday when we were over at Alyn's house that they think you're getting to be a big snob, now that you're on the varsity."

That really made me angry. It just so happens I wasn't at Alyn's on Sunday cause that was the day we visited Daddy at the hospital, and I thought it was pretty lousy of my friends to talk about me behind my back.

But I didn't tell Jenny that, cause when Alyn called Sunday to invite me over, I just told her I had to train and couldn't make it.

The reason I didn't mention the hospital thing

was cause it's none of anyone else's business about Daddy, and I knew if I told Alyn about the visit, everyone would find out and ask me how he was. And I don't like other people prying into my private life.

But instead of going into all this with Jenny, I just told her, "Talk for yourself if you have anything to say to me about our friendship, and leave Rachel and Sammy and everyone else out of it."

"I can't figure you out anymore, Stevie. I'm just trying to be friends. We *are* supposed to be best friends, in case you've forgotten."

I guess I wasn't thinking right when I said, "Just butt out, Jenny, and mind your own business. And don't give me this stuff about being best friends, 'cause we're just not anymore!"

I don't know what made me say that. I was sorry right after I said it. But then it was too late to take it back, cause Jenny started crying and ran ahead to get away from me.

Sixteen

Well, maybe Jenny was right that running is the most important thing in my life. Anyway, the most important thing in my life right now is that I'm ready for the race tomorrow. At least I think I am.

My ankle is all better. When I first started running on it again, I used a special bandage that's like an ace bandage, only it's fitted to your ankle. But then I stopped using it, cause my track coach, Mrs. Mackley, said my ankle won't get stronger if I give it too much support after it's better.

Grandma's not too sure it's a good idea to take the bandage off yet, but I showed her how the swelling is down and how I'm not limping or anything, and she seemed OK about it after that. She just said, "I never know what you kids will be doing next. In my day, girls didn't even go out for sports the way you youngsters do today." It must've been the pits to be a girl in Grandma's day.

I haven't broken my training schedule once in the last two weeks, and my times are the best they've ever been. I've never wanted to win anything so badly as this race in my life. I really feel up for it. I just hope I can run my best tomorrow, cause I'm sure I can take first for the team if I can run my best time. Mrs. Mackley told me that the fastest time recorded for the best girl I'll be running against at the meet is 19.27 seconds, which is Jill Johnson from Somerset's time in the 3.2 cross-country. My best time is almost half a minute less.

Mrs. Mackley obviously believes I'm going to win, cause I saw on her score sheet where she adds up the points she thinks we'll get before each meet that she gave me one point, which means first place, for the event. It'd be awful to let her down, and the rest of the team too.

The scoring in cross-country meets is different from winter or spring track. In cross-country the team with the lowest amount of points wins. If you come in first, you get one point, second two points, and so on. Each team is allowed at most five winning places, so even if you run all seven varsity team members, only five places count. A shut-out score would be 15–40, with the winning team having only fifteen points. It takes a little getting used to.

Mrs. Mackley's score sheet shows a really close meet, with our team supposedly winning by just a couple of points less than the second place team. According to Mrs. Mackley, Somerset will place second, with twenty-nine points to our twenty-seven.

For dinner tonight I made a whole big pot of spaghetti and ate it with sauce and parmesan cheese. It's what runners call "carbohydrate-packing." Carbohydrates give you lots of energy for the race the next day. Robby thinks it's dumb and unscientific, but he doesn't read *Runner's World* like I do. All the big runners like Grete Waitz from Norway, who's won all those marathons and set a whole bunch of world records, carbo-pack before racing.

After dinner I made a list and titled it, "Ten reasons why I want to win." This is how my list came out:

1. CAUSE I LIKE WINNING.
2. SO I'LL BE THE YOUNGEST GIRL IN MY SCHOOL EVER TO WIN THE 3.2 CROSS-COUNTRY FOR THE VARSITY.
3. SO MY TEAM WILL WIN THE MEET.
4. SO I CAN QUALIFY FOR THE ALL-EASTERN IN THE SPRING.
5. SO I CAN SHOW BETH KILE, WHO TOLD DEBBIE SELIGMAN SHE DIDN'T THINK I'D BEAT THE SOMERSET GIRL, HOW MUCH BETTER I CAN DO THAN SHE DID LAST YEAR. SHE LOST BY HOURS.
6. FOR MRS. MACKLEY.

7. TO IMPRESS JEB GRAY.
8. SO MY PICTURE WILL BE TAKEN FOR THE SCHOOL PAPER AND MY NAME LISTED FOR BEING THE FRONT-RUNNER AT THE MEET.
9. CAUSE I HATE LOSING.
10. SO DADDY WILL LIVE.

I crossed out number ten cause it doesn't really make sense. It's just a kind of game I play in my head lately when I'm training. I tell myself that if I can beat yesterday's time, Daddy will live, and if I can't he'll die. Then I push really hard so I can run as fast as possible so I can save his life. Sometimes, if I think I'm not going to make it at the last minute, I change what I have to do, so Daddy doesn't have to die.

But I know it's a stupid, superstitious thing to do and that it has nothing really to do with whether Daddy will make it or not. There's no way anyone can control that.

Sometimes I get so caught up with playing the game that it ruins the whole run for me. I keep adding new things to what I have to do. Like if I run from this tree to that stream in fifteen seconds by my timer watch, Daddy won't die. Or if I leap over a log and land three feet ahead and keep running without falling, Daddy will live. Sometimes I feel like my mind is going crazy, but I can't make myself stop.

Just before I was going to bed, the phone rang,

and it was Jenny calling to wish me good luck tomorrow. I was really happy when I heard her voice again, and it made me realize Jenny really is my best friend. She deserves to be since she's a big enough person to do that after what I said to her.

I didn't exactly apologize for the other day, but I did read her my list, which was kind of like making up with her.

I left out my reason number ten for wanting to win, which I was too embarrassed to read her. But even though I crossed it out with a line through it and didn't read it to Jenny, I still think it'll be on my mind tomorrow when I run my race.

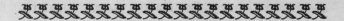

Seventeen

I lost my race in the track meet last Saturday. Right after I passed the two-mile marker, I started playing the game in my head of saving Daddy's life. But I was having trouble concentrating, cause I kept thinking, "This is ridiculous, Stevie. You can't control life and death."

I looked around and suddenly realized that I was ahead of Jill Johnson by about fifty yards and that I was going to win for sure. And that was when it happened. My mind went crystal clear—it just kind of stopped still—and I could actually feel myself slow down for the thought that was coming.

I knew I was going to win, and I knew at the

same exact instant that Daddy was going to die. And suddenly what I was doing seemed ridiculous. Like there was no purpose to my racing anymore, since winning wouldn't make a difference.

Then I felt Jill come up behind me, and then beside me, and then pass me, and I put on a spurt to catch her. That was when my foot caught in a little trench or a low place along the trail. I stumbled and fell, and since Jill was way ahead when I looked up, I just lay there not moving until the next runner passed me.

Nothing was hurting, and I could've picked myself up and kept going, but I didn't. I don't know why exactly. I guess I wanted first, and if I couldn't have it, I wasn't going to try anymore. And also I know I wanted to win so Daddy would live, and when I suddenly realized he was going to die anyway, second or third place didn't mean anything. I just kind of gave up and didn't care anymore.

On Monday Daddy died of a blood clot, which is called an embolism. Time doesn't seem to go by since Daddy died, cause six days later I feel as sad and empty as the day I came home from school and Grandma and Papa-La were here and Mom took me up to her room to tell me that Daddy died while I was in French class. She didn't say that he died while I was in French class. She said he died at ten fifteen that morning, which would've been just about when I was taking our weekly French quiz on conjugations.

The verb *courir*, which means "to run," was on our list, and it would've been amazingly ironic if just when Daddy was dying I was conjugating the verb *courir*. I can never remember if the imperfect has one r or two.

Imperfect. That's what life is. It's all wrong that Daddy died. I'm not nearly old enough to have no father. Your father's supposed to die when you're grown-up, like when Alyn's mother's father died last year. He was eighty-four. Daddy is—was—only forty. Alyn still has her father, and I'll have to live all the rest of my life without mine. It's just not fair.

I remember how after Mom told me that Daddy was dead, I went into my room and lay on my bed looking out the window at the same silver maple Daddy could see through his window. I kept getting stuck on a really illogical thought, that it didn't make sense for me to be able to see the tree anymore if Daddy couldn't.

The whole feeling reminded me of how strange it seemed the day after our dog Windy died, and I walked outside and saw some dog-do in the yard. It seemed impossible that his dog-do could still be around and he was dead. I was only seven when Windy died. Half as old as I am now.

I also remember the weird way it felt later on the day that Daddy died when they called me down from my room to have something to eat. Grandma brought one of her coffee cakes with shredded almonds all over the top, and it tasted the same good way it always does. And that didn't seem right either. I always thought you couldn't taste anything after someone you love dies.

I didn't put butter on my cake this time, though. Something made me feel that it wouldn't be right to use butter or eat chocolate pudding or candy or anything else you loved the day someone died.

It made me think about how some of the Catholic kids at school don't eat meat during Lent because of Christ dying so they could be saved.

What really amazes me is that I still do a lot of things the same even though Daddy's gone and won't be coming back. I eat and sleep and take baths and wash my hair and go outside and look at television. I even laugh when something's funny.

But one thing that's different is that I'm not running anymore, at least not yet. I guess I feel it wouldn't be the right thing to go off and run now. Even though sometimes I feel like I'd like to. Maybe I think it wouldn't be right because people are still coming over to make condolence calls.

Of course I didn't go to Beth's party Friday night. I wouldn't have wanted to go anyway, even if it hadn't been during the first week when Daddy died and while lots of people were still coming to the house to visit.

I don't really want to see my friends or the kids at

school, but Mom says tomorrow, which is Monday, will be a week, and it will be time for Robby and me to go back to school.

I know I'll be embarrassed to have to face everyone. I was even embarrassed when Jenny came over with her parents the other night. I just didn't know what to say or how to act.

I hate it when people tell you how sorry they are that your father died. Like when Debra Maxwell saw me outside yesterday while she was riding her bike past the house, she stopped and made a big production out of telling me she heard the news and how sorry she felt. I'm sure she rode by the house on purpose just to see if I look any different now.

What are you supposed to say, anyway? It's not like when you're taught to say, "How do you do," when you meet someone and shake their hand. No one tells you what to say when someone consoles you for your father dying.

You can't just say "Thanks," cause what are you thanking them for? Their feeling sorry? That's stupid. I feel like saying, "Oh, that's OK," cause I don't want people to fuss over me and feel sorry for me and treat me like a poor orphan. But you can't say, "Oh, it's OK," when your father just died, cause it's not OK and it never will be OK again.

It's hardest of all to really believe Daddy's never coming back. I know in my head he's not. I saw him buried in a coffin under the ground, so I know he's dead and can't ever come back to life again. But I imagine a lot that he's not dead. Just off somewhere very sick where he doesn't want us to see him suffering. And then I imagine that he'll get better someday and come back to us all healthy again.

At night I pray to God that if he makes everything better again, makes it all like it was before, I won't be the way I used to be. I'll be more considerate of other people and try not to fight with Robby, and if Daddy doesn't feel well I'll go up to his room, and spend some time with him, instead of always doing my own things.

But I know it's all useless, cause there's no way to change what happened. And anyway, even if God could fix things after they go wrong, which He can't, He probably wouldn't listen to my prayers because I've never really prayed before. Except when Windy died and I asked God to bring him back. But you can't use God just for emergencies.

When I'm in bed at night before I fall asleep, I listen for Daddy's footsteps. I listen for the sound of his feet falling on the tiles downstairs. Footfalls. Daddy's footfalls. I'll never forget that sound— different from the sound of anyone else walking on that floor. I always know—knew—when it was Daddy walking there, no matter who else was in the house.

I play a game at night of pretending everything's all right and none of this ever happened. That we're just a normal family like Beth's or Sammy's or Jenny's. I can only play the game when I'm all alone, because if I'm with people they act as though Daddy just died and then I can't pretend he didn't.

But I don't think I should play the game anymore, because when I stop playing and have to start remembering that it really is true that Daddy's dead and gone forever, I can barely stand it I feel so sad and miss him so much and want him back more than I've ever wanted anything in my whole entire life. Much more than I wanted to win at East Bradley. Much, much, much more than I even wanted Windy back.

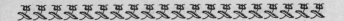

Eighteen

This winter is never going to end. I've already had one strep throat and the flu. We've had freezing cold weather for so long that the pipes froze last night, and when we woke up this morning we had no water. After the first couple times we flushed the toilets, you couldn't get them to flush anymore cause of there being no running water in the pipes. And it's still only the beginning of January, so we have at least two more months of winter.

Mom called the plumber while we were having breakfast, and he told her he was so busy fixing frozen pipes that he was out working 'til eleven last night. He told her he couldn't get to our house 'til—at the very earliest—the end of the afternoon and maybe not 'til tomorrow.

When Mom got off the phone, the English muffins in the toaster oven were burned, and she got so upset she actually started crying. She's like that a lot lately.

She also gets angry at me and Robby for absolutely nothing. Even little stuff she used to not care about, like if I fold the towel the wrong way after my shower and forget to pick up the mat and hang it over the side of the tub.

Part of the reason I've been feeling so crummy lately is cause I haven't been getting any exercise, at least not enough. I decided not to go out for winter track, cause I really can't stand some of the girls on the team, like snotty Beth Kile and Debbie Seligman.

Anyway, running's not the only thing that matters, even though a lot of kids go around acting like it is. It's really repulsive the way all they do is talk about running all the time.

Jenny once asked me if the reason I wasn't going out for winter track was because of what happened at East Bradley and my not qualifying for the All-Eastern. I told her that had nothing to do with anything. I just don't care about running anymore the way I used to.

School stinks this year. I even hate English, which was my favorite subject last year, cause my teacher, Miss Yamaguchi, is the worst teacher I've ever had.

She gives the most ridiculous assignments, like writing a modern version of a Shakespeare play. And then when you write one, she tells you it's not as good as Shakespeare did it. At least that's what I got from her comment on my play, which said, "Ophelia is really much more complex than you make her seem." If she wants Ophelia to be like Shakespeare made her, then why doesn't she just go read *Hamlet*?

Another thing which shows how dumb Miss Yamaguchi is and how small her mind is, is what she did with a word I used on my last composition.

The assignment was to write a story about a character who was changed by some very memorable event that happened in his or her life. It could be a good or bad event that made the person change.

I wrote about a character who was a runner who used to think running was the most important thing in the world and then realized, through a memorable experience she had, that it wasn't. The memorable experience was when the girl in my story falls and loses a big race and comes in in last place.

In my story I used the word "footfalls" to describe something about the girl's running stride. Miss Yamaguchi crossed it out with a real big X mark over it and wrote in the margin of my paper, "I believe the technical running term that you want here is 'foot-plant.' See dictionary for meaning of 'footfalls.'"

Can you believe it? Miss Yamaguchi probably

never even ran around the block in her whole life, but she thinks she's an expert on running terms!

Anyway, I *did* look up "footfalls" in the dictionary, and it means exactly what I meant when I used it in my story. I wanted to describe the way feet sound when they strike the ground.

How are writers supposed to be creative if they're not allowed to use words the way they want?

My report card this winter was pretty bad. In fact, my grades were so much worse than first quarter that I got a note in my box to go see the guidance counselor Mrs. Durce. So now I have to see her once a week until my grades get better.

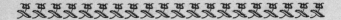

Nineteen

I hate Miss Yamaguchi. I've never hated a teacher so much, especially an English teacher. I used to hate the guidance counselor, Mrs. Durce, but now that I'm getting to know her a little better, I realize she's very nice and understands kids much better than most grown-ups do.

Today when I was in Mrs. Durce's office I told her how much I hate Miss Yamaguchi. She asked me why, and I told her about the outside reading list and how we're supposed to put down the names of books we read on our own on a list. The more books you read, the more extra credit you get. You can write down comments about the book if you

99

want to, but you don't have to and no one does except Philip Rudy and Hazel Friedkin.

Miss Yamaguchi keeps all the lists together in alphabetical order in a ring binder on her desk, and everyone can see what everyone else writes down. You're not supposed to look—it's part of the Honor System—but everyone does.

Some of the boys even put things on other people's list. I'm sure that's how *Lolita* turned up on Patty Miller's list, cause she swore she didn't put it there and knowing Patty Miller, who's the biggest prude in ninth grade, I'm sure she didn't.

I know some kids even lie about what they read, cause there's no way Lynn Bespaloff—who's practically retarded—could possibly understand Dostoyevsky, and I saw *Crime and Punishment* on her list.

I told Mrs. Durce that I put *A Little Princess* down three times on my list, and Miss Yamaguchi crossed all three times off and said in her snotty way that I was capable of more advanced reading.

She also said I wasn't "fulfilling my potential." Teachers at Wakefield School love that expression. When I was younger, I used to think "potential" was a kind of jar, and if you were good yours was full, and if you weren't it was empty. I always thought mine must be in between, since my grades were mostly B's and B pluses.

It really made me furious when Miss Yamaguchi

did that. If she wanted to cross off two of the times cause they were repeats, that might've been fair, but she wouldn't even let me count it once.

Just cause fat Philip Rudy and Hazel Friedkin read these big, huge books no one else reads 'til college doesn't mean everyone has to read that stuff. Even Mom says outside reading should be what you *like* reading, and I like *A Little Princess*.

What's even more unfair is what Miss Yamaguchi told Philip Rudy the other day when he was showing off and reading *Ulysses* before class started. Everyone's hanging around and talking and stuff, and there's fat Philip sitting on the window ledge with this book that's almost as fat as he is. And then Miss Yamaguchi goes over to him and says real loud so everyone can hear and be impressed, "My, what a challenging literary work, Philip. Since *Ulysses* is so long, you can put each part of it down as one book credit on your list." What barf!

Then Mrs. Durce asked me why I like *A Little Princess* so much that I keep reading it over and over. You could tell by the way she asked that she didn't think there was anything wrong with reading books lots of times if you like them.

I told her the story of the little girl Sarah who goes from being the richest girl at boarding school to an absolute orphan when her father dies, and then she has to be a scullery maid and loses her beautiful room and all her fine things. And then at the end her father's best friend comes and saves her by making her rich and happy again.

"Do you like the little girl Sarah in the story, Stevie?" Mrs. Durce asked me. I told her I like her a lot, and when she asked me why, I said, "Because she's so brave when she gets poor and her father dies. She just keeps acting the same as she always did—nice to everyone and kind of proud, like she's not going to let it get to her that everything's different and horrible now."

Then Mrs. Durce said something which I never thought of. "You know, Stevie, as you tell me about Sarah, I'm reminded a little bit of you. Do you think you've ever felt like Sarah?"

I had to think a real long time about her question before I could answer it. At first I almost said no, I didn't think I ever felt that way, but the longer I thought about it, the more I thought that maybe I did feel a little like Sarah.

I didn't exactly want to tell Mrs. Durce that I felt like that, and I had one of those lumps in your throat that make it hard to talk or even swallow. So I just sort of nodded.

Mrs. Durce said a very nice thing then which made me feel real good. She leaned across her desk toward me and sort of whispered instead of talked what she was saying, "You know, Stevie, I wouldn't say this to many ninth-graders, because I don't know if they could understand this as well as I think you will."

Mrs. Durce stopped talking for a minute and looked very straight at me, so I kind of had to look right back at her. I could feel myself begin to blush, and I had to look away. Then she started talking again.

"Sometimes, Stevie, grown-ups miss the point of what kids are doing. And I think what happened with Miss Yamaguchi may be one of those times. I think she just didn't understand what you've been feeling since your father died, and she didn't understand how important reading *A Little Princess* is to you right now. Because if she had understood this, she would never have hurt your feelings by not giving you credit for Sarah's story."

I asked Mrs. Durce if she thought I should put the book back on the list, and she said she thought that might expose me to being hurt again.

Then she took a piece of paper out of her desk and wrote something across the top of it, underlined what she wrote, and turned the page around for me to see. It said, in big, block letters in red ink—Mrs. Durce always writes in red ink— "STEVIE'S STORIES—THE ONES I READ BECAUSE I WANT TO."

As I looked at the page, Mrs. Durce was telling me that we could keep this special list in her desk, where no one but the two of us would see it, and she promised me that whatever I wrote on it would never get crossed out.

It seemed a little bit like a silly kind of thing to

do, but I could tell Mrs. Durce was trying to be nice, and I didn't want to say anything to make her feel bad. I also was feeling pretty good about her telling me I was more understanding than a lot of ninth-graders.

Twenty

Jenny invited me to sleep over at her house this coming Saturday night. At first I wasn't sure if I wanted to go, cause I haven't felt much like being around there lately. But Jenny's older sister Gwenn is having a party, and Jenny was almost sure Jeb Gray would be there, cause Gwenn and Jeb are both juniors and hang around with a lot of the same kids.

The thing that gets me about being around Jenny's house these days is the way her mother treats me. Ever since Daddy got real sick the night of my party and went to the hospital for the last time, Mrs. Pryor always asks me in this super concerned kind of way, "How are things going at home, Stevie?"

It's not the same kind of way parents always ask their kids' friends how things are going. With Mrs. Pryor you get the impression she thinks she's on some kind of inside track that runs right through our family's private life. The last time I was over there she asked me how Robby was "adjusting." That really bugged me a lot. She makes it sound like we're living through some sort of tragic soap opera.

Anyway, I decided that I'd sleep over there on Saturday cause there'll be so much going on, with Gwenn's party and all, that Mrs. Pryor probably won't have time to go into her usual routine with me.

Saturday night at Jenny's didn't really go too well. Beth Kile and Debbie Seligman, the two most obnoxious girls on the running team, were both there. At first they acted like Jenny and I didn't exist.

Then at one point Jen and I went over to fill our cups with Coke at the table where all the food and drinks were laid out, and Beth said in this real loud voice so everyone standing around could hear, "Wouldn't you kids rather be watching 'Little House on the Prairie'?"

Then Debbie, who acts like Beth's shadow when

it comes to being snotty and stuck up, said, "My little sister's into 'Bionic Woman.' I bet the freshman set still digs that stuff."

That really made me furious, cause Debbie's sister's this tiny little kid around nine or ten years old. And just as Debbie was saying it, Jeb Gray came over and stood right next to me and started helping himself to a handful of potato chips. I thought I'd die of embarrassment.

When I looked over at him, he winked and said, "Don't let them bug you, Stevie. Beth's just jealous cause when she tried out for the original Bionic Woman part, they gave the role to someone more qualified."

Everyone standing around started laughing really loud when Jeb said that, but I could feel my face getting all red from feeling so self-conscious.

I didn't know what to do with myself, but I sure didn't want to stand around blushing, so I leaned over to take some more soda, and then I did the most embarrassing thing I've ever done. I spilled the whole bottle of Coke all over the table. When I reached out to pick the bottle up, I got Coke all over the sleeve of my white turtleneck.

When I saw what a horrible mess I was making, I didn't know whether to cry or run out of the room. I think if it hadn't been for Jeb, who just kind of took over and got everything all fixed up, I would've made an even worse fool of myself in front of everyone.

Jeb grabbed a pile of napkins and threw them real quick on the puddle of soda that was about to run over the edge of the table. Then some of the other kids started pitching in and helping move the stuff that'd gotten wet. I started helping too.

At one point Jeb's and my arms kind of brushed together, and he turned and smiled this real sweet smile at me. "You OK now, Stevie?" he asked, and I said, "Thanks for the help, Jeb."

Then he said real quietly so only I could hear, "If I rescued you from a sprained ankle, I guess I can rescue you from a little Coke. Come on, let's get away from here before something else happens."

Then Jeb sort of put his arm around me and steered me away from the table and toward the door leading out to the back porch. As we were walking he was saying that he hoped my nice sweater wouldn't be stained from the Coke.

Jenny's house has this porch room that they put screens around in the summertime, and then when it's winter they replace them with glass windows. It's kind of neat in the winter cause they just leave outdoor-type furniture in there all the time. When it's cold they keep this Franklin stove going that burns wood, so it feels a little like you're outside at a campsite.

At least that's what Jen and I would pretend when we were younger and used to sleep out in the porch room in sleeping bags. We had a silly joke about the Franklin stove, which we used to call "Frankie." If the fire was getting low, one of us would say, "Frankie's burning out," and the other one would answer, "Just like Franklin Caldwell." Mr. Caldwell is the principal of the Lower School, and since he's so old and almost ready to retire, everyone's always saying he's all burned out. Whenever we'd tell the "Frankie" joke, Jen and I would get hysterical laughing like it was the funniest thing in the world. It doesn't seem so funny anymore.

When Jeb and I got out to the porch room, the first thing he said was, "Hey, this fireplace looks really neat, Stevie. Let's sit by it for a while and get away from all the noise in there."

As soon as we were sitting there on the floor in front of the Franklin stove, I began to get this really uncomfortable feeling. Jeb was sitting so close to me that I felt all scrunched up. I wanted to move a little to make myself more comfortable, but before I had a chance to figure out how to do it, Jeb put his arm around me.

Our backs were facing the door that led back into the part of the house where the other kids were, and I kept worrying that someone like Beth or Debbie would walk by and see us.

At one point when I looked around toward the door, I saw that someone—maybe it was Jeb as we came in—had brought the door to, so that it wasn't really closed tight, but kids walking by outside the porch room wouldn't be able to see us. That's when I realized Jeb was probably going to try something with me.

When Jeb saw me look back at the door, he said,

"Don't sweat it about Beth Kile. She just thinks she's hot stuff since you stopped running and she's the fastest girl on the team again."

It really amazed me that Jeb Gray knew I wasn't taking winter track. Then he said, "You really should go out for the team again, Stevie. You could give old Bionic Beth a real run for her money!" We both laughed when Jeb said that, and I began to feel a little more at ease.

Then I felt his arm tighten around my shoulder. I could hear a Billy Joel song playing in the other room, and I got that nervous feeling again that someone might see us.

Suddenly I felt a kind of pang of missing something or someone, and I started wishing real hard that instead of this scene with Jeb happening, Jenny and I could be out here again having one of our sleepover dates where we pretended to be camping out.

As I was thinking this, Jeb tried to kiss me. He sort of turned himself toward me while he was trying to reach my mouth, but I guess I did something wrong, and the kiss half missed my mouth and landed mostly on my cheek. I just automatically turned toward the door again.

"Don't be nervous, Stevie. No one's coming out here." Then before I could move away, Jeb put his other arm around me and began to pull me closer to him. This time when he kissed me he made sure to kiss my mouth, but maybe cause he was holding me so tight, the kiss felt a little too hard.

Just then the absolute worst thing happened. The door flew open and Mrs. Pryor walked right in on us. She must've been so shocked to catch us kissing that she didn't know what to say. So she just spun around real fast and left the room, but as she left she flicked on the light, which had been off the whole time, and she left the door wide open behind her.

That kind of broke up the whole scene between Jeb and me. And anyway, some other kids were starting to come out to the porch room, so Jeb and I just moved away from each other. I didn't see him again that evening, cause a few minutes after that happened I went and found Jenny and told her I was tired and felt like going up to bed.

Even though I wanted really badly to tell Jenny about what happened with Jeb, I felt kind of confused about saying anything cause of her mother walking in on us. I thought maybe Jenny'd be mad at me for letting her mom see us doing that.

So I wound up just keeping the whole incident to myself, and the next morning, very early, before the rest of the house was up, I got dressed and left for home. Since Jenny was still sleeping, I wrote a note and taped it to her mirror telling her I had to get home cause it was my turn to walk Biscuit.

Even though at my age I could never admit this to anyone, I actually felt a little homesick. As I was walking toward our house, I started thinking about how good it would feel to crawl into my own bed again.

When I got to the driveway, I could tell Mom and Robby were still sleeping, cause the shades on their windows were still pulled down. So I let myself in real quietly and went up to my room, kicked off my Reeboks, and got under the covers with all my clothes still on.

As soon as I closed my eyes to try to fall asleep, I could feel them filling up with tears. I turned my head into the pillow so when the crying started no one would hear. It happens like that all the time lately. I just keep thinking of Daddy and how much better things would be if he were here.

I wonder when I'll really begin to like being kissed. I don't mean like the *idea* of being kissed, but actually like the *feeling* of being kissed.

On Tuesday when I told Mrs. Durce what happened with Jeb, she said, "To everything there is a season, and your time will come, Stevie. Just you wait and see."

I don't know why exactly, but I almost couldn't bring myself to tell her about Mrs. Pryor walking in on us. Then I took a plunge and just blurted it out, and I'm really glad I did, cause what she said made me feel a lot better about the whole thing.

"You know, Stevie," Mrs. Durce said, "I don't think Jenny's mom was so shocked by seeing two young people kissing. I bet she was just naturally a little embarrassed by taking you by surprise like that."

I didn't know what to say then, but I know I must've looked amazed, cause Mrs. Durce smiled a real big smile and said in her nice, kidding kind of way, "Come, come, Stevie. Don't forget that Mrs. Pryor was once kissed for the very first time too."

Something else Mrs. Durce said when I was in her office really stuck with me. After I told her how I felt when Jeb was kissing me, she said that sometimes, after an experience as powerful as losing your father, a girl may lock up feelings for a while just to keep them safe from getting hurt again. I think I know what she means.

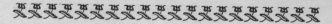

Twenty-One

When I got home this afternoon, Robby was in a twit about his social studies term paper.

He was standing in the middle of the living room floor with all the pages laid out on every inch of rug and all over every piece of furniture. He was smack in the middle of all the papers when I came in, and he was having a fit cause he couldn't find a way to get something he wanted without stepping on the pages.

When I saw what was going on, I got hysterical laughing. It was about the funniest thing I've ever seen in my whole life.

Naturally Robby got angry at me for laughing, and I could tell he was about to fly into one of his rages, cause he was already so hassled about the report.

I decided to be a good kid and ask him if I could help by getting him the thing he needed. He said it was a letter from the Governor's office and that it was upstairs on his desk. As I was coming back downstairs with the letter, I looked it over but couldn't figure out what it was about.

"Hey, Robby, what are all these boxes that are checked off here, and how come you got this?"

"It's for my social studies report on Making a Contribution to Our Environment. My project is to help clean up the industrial pollution in North Jersey."

"You mean that mess we always smell on the Turnpike when we drive up to New York?" I asked him. "That's going to take a lot of cleaning up!"

"Yaa. Well, everyone had to choose some environmental problem and try to make it better by taking 'Positive Action.' Mr. Helgeson says even kids can change the world if they really try."

"How idealistic can you get? But what does this letter have to do with your project, Robby?"

"Oh, that. I did a whole bunch of research on ways of cleaning up the pollution problem. I even interviewed Danny Klein's father, cause he's an environmental engineer at Rutgers. Then I wrote this whole big outline of my ideas to the Governor, and all I got back is that dumb letter. Now I can't say in my report that I made a contribution, cause all the letter proves is that no one liked my ideas."

"Were you expecting them to?" I asked him.

"Well, Mr. Helgeson said he wants the projects to have what he calls 'Impact.' I'll probably get a D minus on mine."

I know Robby was really upset, but I couldn't help thinking how funny the letter was, and I started laughing again.

Just as Robby was about to get mad, I said, "Hey, this could be a great way to end your report. No kidding, Robby. Look at this . . ."

I held the letter out to show him how ridiculous it was. This is exactly what the letter said:

Dear Mr. Farr:
Your letter of April 16, 1982, has been sent to this office for reply. This office is well aware of the conditions of emissions along the New Jersey Turnpike. It is extremely polluted in certain areas. Steps are being taken to correct this situation; they are as follows:

Then there was a whole list with boxes next to it of actions that were supposedly already being taken to solve the problem, and some of them were checked off.

The letter was signed by the Acting Chief of the Bureau of Air Pollution Control, and you just knew he didn't really read Robby's letter.

"Look at these stupid boxes, Robby." I was starting to get real excited about how Robby could write a really great conclusion to his report. "The Governor never even read your ideas. And neither did Chief Big Stench from the Bureau of Air Pollution Control. They don't give a damn what you think, or what anyone else thinks. It just proves they don't give a damn about the problem—"

"I knew I should've chosen another problem to work on."

"No, that's not the point, Robby. You chose a problem cause it needed fixing. And look at what happened. There are some things in life we just can't control, no matter how hard we try. You should tell that in your report, Robby. Instead of all that garbage about how school kids can change the world."

"Maybe you're right, Stevie." Robby was beginning to sound convinced.

"Of course I am. You just tell it like it is. And if Mr. Helgeson doesn't like it, he can take his 'Impact' and shove it."

After that, Robby got so excited he worked all night writing a conclusion that told how he researched all these possible solutions to the problem and how the government wasn't even interested in his ideas.

I really felt good that I helped Robby. When he knocked at my door around eleven o'clock to see if I wanted to hear what he wrote, I felt really proud of myself for getting him going.

Robby's conclusion sounded very serious and grown-up, and you could tell from how he wrote it that he had a lot of deep feelings about what should be done to make New Jersey a better place.

When he was finished reading to me, he flopped down on my bed and said how exhausted he was. He had all the papers from the living room all put together in a royal blue report folder, and he was holding the papers he just read me, which were still on scrap paper, cause he hadn't typed them yet.

I saw how tired he looked and thought it'd be nice to ask him if he wanted me to type the last part for him. He picked himself up real quick from my bed, ran over to my desk where I was sitting, just about jumped on me, and said, "Would you, Stevie, would you really do that?"

I was a little embarrassed cause he was so grateful, and I guess I'm not used to Robby thanking me for things. I took the pages from his hand and said, "Sure. At the rate you type, which is about four words with forty errors per minute, you'd probably miss your deadline."

Robby sat on the edge of my bed and watched me type every word. You could tell he really liked what he wrote, cause each time I pulled a page out of the typewriter, he grabbed it and read it over and over. He kept wanting me to hear things again that I already heard, and I had to tell him to be quiet so I could type it right.

At one point after he was sitting quietly on my

bed for a while, he said, "Stevie, what'd you mean before when you said there are things in life we can't control? I mean, if I worked really hard and got to be a senator someday, then couldn't I fix the environment the way it should be?"

"But right now you can't, Robby, so it's outside of your control. I don't mean you shouldn't try, like you did. I just mean you can't blame yourself for not controlling the situation."

He was quiet again for a while, and then after I typed some more, he asked me, "Are there some things *you* can't control, Stevie?"

I guess Robby's question really must've hit home, cause I said without even stopping to think, "Oh, lots of things, Robby. Like when I lost my race at East Bradley last fall . . . and Daddy's dying."

Robby didn't say anything for a real long time, and I couldn't see his face cause I was typing with my back turned, but I figured he knew what I meant. Then he said in a very low voice so I had to stop typing to hear, "Do you think Daddy would've liked my report, Stevie?"

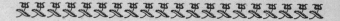

Twenty-Two

I've been running again, and I'm beginning to feel a little better. At least when I'm out running I'm not sitting around feeling sad and sorry for myself.

This morning I got up early and ran along Cedar Brook all the way to the dam down by the old Foreman Estate. When I got to the dam I decided to run back on the other side of Cedar Brook, so I took my track shoes and socks off and waded across.

Because of all the rain we've been having, the brook was overflowing and the water was icy cold but felt very good to walk through. I even scooped some up in my hand to wash my face, which was all sweaty from running, and then I got down on my knees and drank some of the water right as it was running in the stream. It was a neat feeling, the water kind of tickling my lips as I drank. My knees got all scratched up from the gravel and rocks on the bank, but it was worth it.

Stream water tastes so much better than tap water. Not tinny or stale or filled with all kinds of gunk that's not supposed to be there. I remember how sometimes when we'd be out driving somewhere in the country, Daddy would say how beautiful nature was and how if God had meant for it to be filled with chemicals and pollution, he'd have put them there in the first place.

Daddy loved the outdoors. He loved to walk and walk for miles and miles. Mom always used to tell stories about how Daddy would drag me on these really long walks when I was a tiny little girl and how much I loved going with him and how I never complained even though when we got home I was always so tired I couldn't move.

Maybe I loved running because of all those walks with Daddy. Footfalls. Daddy's and mine together. And now my own.

After I finished drinking from the stream, I wanted my feet to dry off a little before I put my socks and track shoes back on. So I found a place on the ground that wasn't too muddy, and I was just sitting very still like that when suddenly the most amazing thing happened. Right out of the trees from behind me a big deer and two little baby deer came flying out and down to the stream. It really was like flying the way they moved so gracefully and silently.

They crossed the stream hardly making a splash, and when they got to the other side they kind of planted themselves on the muddy slope, and all three of them began drinking from the stream.

I was so close I could see their little noses, like tiny horse muzzles, moving as they kind of sucked up the water without making any noise. I guess deer don't lap up water the way dogs do.

Then the mother deer, it must've been the mother cause it didn't have antlers or anything, picked her head up from the stream and put her mouth real near the rump of one of the babies. I couldn't see if she touched her mouth to the little deer or not—it seemed like she must have made some sound or touch as a signal—and then they all turned toward the trees on the other side of the brook and bolted away. I'm sure they never knew I was so near and that a person was watching them.

As they ran away, I realized it was a family of three—a mother and her two children—traveling through the woods on their own with no father. Animal fathers don't usually stay with their young, I don't think. And I suddenly got this amazingly powerful pang of sadness. It was almost like a physical pain. I felt it deep inside my chest, and I can even feel it now, like a soreness after a wound.

Then I put my shoes on and ran home, on the

other side of Cedar Brook from the side I ran on coming to the dam.

I must've run a total of almost eight or nine miles, I think, cause I started at six thirty and I didn't get home 'til eight fifteen. I figure I must be running around seven-and-a-half- to eight-minute cross-country miles, even allowing for being out of condition. And I don't think I was wading and sitting for more than half an hour at the most.

If I hadn't lost my temper and broken the pedometer Daddy got me for my birthday, I would've been able to clock my mileage on my own. At the time I broke it, a pedometer felt like a pretty cheap substitute for a father.

I guess I felt cheated cause Daddy always promised he'd take me out in the car to clock miles, and something always came up so we couldn't do it. And then he got too sick to do it anymore. And then he died. I think I might not have broken the pedometer if only Daddy had just been able to give it to me himself. It wasn't the same getting it from Mom.

But I'm sorry now I broke the pedometer. I realize it was the most Dad could do for me, and I should've kept it as a lasting memento. Actually, now it's a kind of lasting memory instead, and maybe that's the way it was meant to be.

Like Daddy. I can remember everything about him, and I know I always will because I'll never let myself forget. But I can't touch or feel him anymore, and I won't ever be able to again.

It's kind of symbolic—the thing about a meter to clock myself with. I was all caught up with running faster, while Daddy was caught up with time running out on him. It's not that I didn't realize his time was running out, it's that I didn't want to take the time to slow down and notice.

Mrs. Durce says that's a natural way for someone the age I was to be, but I wish I could've let Daddy know I knew . . . I wish I could've slowed down enough to tell him, just once before he died, that I loved him and would miss him when he was gone. I wonder if that's why I let myself, maybe I even *made* myself, slow down and lose the race. Kind of like I was punishing myself for letting Daddy slip away. But in a way—maybe because Daddy was so sick and seemed so far away at the end—it felt almost as though he was gone before he died.

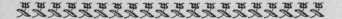

Twenty-Three

I've decided to go out for spring track. Mostly because I need the exercise. I'm not real interested in competing and trying to be the fastest runner on the team anymore. I've kind of stopped thinking I want to be a marathon racer like Grete Waitz when I'm older. I may decide to be a guidance counselor instead, so I can help people understand their feelings. I think I could be good at that.

I guess I realized when I started running again this spring that I just like the way I feel when I run. And this winter, when I wasn't running, I felt awful the whole time. I think you can miss something you're used to doing, just like you can miss someone you're used to being with.

The other day after spring track sign-up, I was walking back to my locker to get my stuff to go home, and Jeb Gray came over and asked me if I was going out for the team. He must've known I was, cause why else would I be at the sign-up? It was the first time Jeb and I really talked since the night at Jenny's. After that we kind of avoided each other, and then Jeb and Beth Kile started to get real hot and heavy for a while toward the end of the winter.

Everyone at school was talking and teasing about their relationship, cause Beth's a senior and Jeb's just a junior. The word was out that he was in it mostly for thrills, cause supposedly Beth's had lots of experience.

I can't figure out how Jeb could've stood old Bionic Beth, but obviously he got tired of her cause Gwenn told Jenny they had a big breakup scene at some party a few weeks ago.

When I told Jeb I *was* going out for spring track, he actually looked glad. Then he said, "You didn't miss much this winter, cause indoor track is mostly workouts and boring stuff you can do inside."

Even though it's not exactly true, I said, "Yaa, I know what you mean. That's why I didn't go out for winter track."

"Have you done any running lately?" he asked, and I told him I've been running a little along Cedar Brook behind where I live.

Then he asked me if I'd like to run with him

sometime over the weekend. Before I even had time to think of how to answer, I just blurted out, "Oh I'd love to!" And then I felt like a jerk for being so un-cool.

But he didn't seem to notice, cause he said right away after that, "How about if I run by your house Saturday morning around eleven, and we do ten K's along Cedar Brook?"

I've noticed how serious runners like Jeb measure distance in kilometers, which they call "K's" for short. I think it sounds neat when they do that.

I felt like saying something about the eight-to-nine-mile run I did the other day along Cedar Brook and up to the old Foreman Estate, but I can't do conversions from miles to kilometers in my head.

So instead I just said, "Ten K's on Saturday would be fine," and then before I could ask him if he knew where my house was, he said, "Greato, see you then," and was off running back in the other direction where the sign-ups were held.

As I was walking home, I remembered back to the way Jeb looked that day last fall at East Bradley when I sprained my ankle and he took his shirt off and his hair was all mussed. Then I thought about the night we kissed at Jenny's house and Mrs. Pryor walked in. Looking back made me realize how much more grown-up I am now than I was then.

I also remembered what Mrs. Durce said about

how everything has a season and how my time would come. I guess I was feeling like my time was now.

Jeb and I ran together this morning, I guess he already knew where my house was, cause he showed up at exactly eleven, like he said he would. We did the same run I did by myself the other day—all the way down to the dam and then back again on the other side.

We even stopped for a drink and took our shoes off and waded around in the icy water for a while. Only this time there were no deer. We saw lots of bushes with buds about to break. You could tell what colors the flowers were going to be by the edge of the bud—pink or yellow or white—that showed around the green leaves that held them closed.

Spring is such a beautiful season. I never noticed 'til this year how many different greens you can find in nature in early spring. Some leaves are almost yellow they're so light, and some are dark, dark green. If you squint your eyes at a whole cluster of bushes in the distance, it seems like you're looking through a kaleidoscope all made up of different shades of green.

We were sitting on the bank of the brook and talking about spring track, and Jeb told me the boys' team is facing a very difficult season since they're losing their coach.

I must've looked shocked, cause Jeb said, "You mean you didn't hear what happened with Mr. Desnick last week?" I told him I hadn't heard anything at all. Then he got real excited and told me the story of how someone saw Mr. Desnick leaning up against a tree kissing Gabrielle Morehouse while they were supposedly out running cross-country during practice week.

Whoever saw them made an anonymous phone call to Mrs. Morehouse, Gabriella's mother, and then supposedly Gabriella confessed the truth, and her mother called Mr. Firestone, our principal.

Jeb said Mr. D. was actually fired, but that Mr. Firestone was telling people he quit, so there wouldn't be a big scandal around school. I couldn't believe it'd happened.

Of course I thought right away of that bus ride to East Bradley last fall, but I didn't say a word about that to Jeb, cause I didn't want him to think I let Mr. Desnick do those things to me. I also thought Jeb might wonder if I let Mr. Desnick kiss me, the way Gabriella did.

And then, just as I was thinking all this stuff, Jeb put his arm around me and started to kiss me. At first it was a real soft, light kiss, and then he put his tongue inside my mouth and pushed me back so we were half lying on the bank. My legs were still bent, so I wasn't exactly lying all the way down.

I wasn't too sure what to do with my hands, so I put them up on Jeb's shoulders just kind of lightly.

I kept remembering hobbling around holding his shoulder at East Bradley last fall. And then I thought back on how awkward our first kiss at Jenny's house was. I kept worrying that I was going to have to smile while Jeb was kissing me.

Then Jeb kind of hugged me tighter, which made my arms go around his back, and we kissed in that position for a while. At one point Jeb pulled away from me and looked at me with a really soft, handsome look on his face and said in a kind of kidding voice, "At least I won't lose my job doing this." And then he kissed me again—this time a little harder—and he took one of his arms from around my back and brought it around to the front so he could touch my breast.

I kept remembering our first kiss that night in Jenny's porch room and how Jeb had missed my mouth. I could tell he was much more experienced now than he'd been then. I got kind of nervous when he started touching me and moved his hand away and put it where it'd been around my back. Then he started rubbing my back up and down very gently right over the place where my bra connects in back, and I began to get that really tingly feeling deep down inside and between my legs where I touch myself at night. I was beginning to feel dizzy and out of breath and a little scared of what was happening.

Suddenly Jeb put his hand down by my waist in back, and before I even realized what he was doing, he had slipped it up under my T-shirt and unfastened my bra. I felt it kind of pop open and then got that loose feeling of not having anything binding me on top.

Before I could stop him Jeb was moving his hand over my breasts. I felt the cold of his hand against my skin, and I suddenly really wanted him to stop. I pulled my mouth away from him and said, in a voice that sounded way too loud as it came out, "No, Jeb!" As soon as I said it, he pulled away and stopped.

He took a real deep breath and kind of shook his head and ran a hand through his mussy hair. I noticed how nice and smooth and strong-looking his hand was and realized it was the same one he'd been touching my bare skin with.

Then he lay back flat on his back on the ground and kind of stretched himself out like he was going to start to do sit-ups or something. He closed his eyes and breathed in and out real deep a couple of times, and while his eyes were closed I saw how his running shorts had a big bulge in front where he'd gotten hard. I felt a little nervous, but I knew I could trust him.

Then suddenly Jeb stood up, grabbed my hand, pulled me up, and said, "See if you can catch me, Stevie Farr," and off he went in a sprint back down the trail toward home.

When we got back to my house we'd run so fast we were both out of breath and drenched in sweat, so we sat on the porch kind of dripping and panting for a while. I had that great feeling you get when you're kind of cooking in your own heat after exercising really hard.

Our dog Biscuit, I mean Biscuit the dog, came padding around from the other side of the house, and Jeb gave him a real workout with an old tennis ball he found lying on the porch. Jeb really liked Biscuit. He told me about their Irish setter Rusty who had to be put to sleep cause of heartworms. Jeb looked really sad when he said that, and I could tell he must be a very sensitive person.

Then Jeb said something very special. He looked like he wasn't sure if he was going to say it, as though he needed to find the courage first. But finally he took my hand real gently and said, "I guess I shouldn't be making such a big deal about my dog dying. I mean . . ." and then he stopped as though he'd lost the confidence to say the rest. "I mean, after what you've been through with your father and all . . . that must be *really* tough to deal with."

I was too choked up inside to say anything, but I squeezed his hand that was still holding mine. I wanted to tell him I really appreciated his being so sensitive, cause I really did, but I couldn't find the words. I hope sometime I'll be able to tell him how good what he said made me feel.

Mom must've heard us playing with Biscuit, cause she came out after a couple minutes and saw us sitting there. "How about some lemonade, kids?" she asked, and I felt really good about how nice she was being to one of my friends. When we said we'd like some and she went back inside to get it, I realized I forgot to introduce her to Jeb or him to her. But when she came out, she just handed him a glass and said in this super casual way, "Here you go, Jeb. I'll just leave the pitcher here, Stevie, so you can help yourselves."

I could hardly believe it was *my* mother being so nice. I didn't even think she heard this morning when I said at breakfast that I'd be running with a friend from the track team named Jeb.

Another thing I've noticed is that once in a while lately Mom actually calls me Stevie. I wonder if it's cause she's decided that now that I'm fourteen and a half, I'm old enough to decide for myself what my name should be.

When Jeb left, he said, "I'll call tomorrow, Stevie, for sure," and then he ran off with his funny mussy hair kind of flying around as he ran.

Twenty-Four

I couldn't get to sleep last night, cause I couldn't stop replaying the scene with Jeb by Cedar Brook. I kept imagining it all over and over again and trying to remember everything exactly as it happened, so I could pretend it was happening again.

I started touching myself and imagining that the hand I was touching myself with was Jeb's. I began touching my breast—the same one Jeb touched—and I felt the nipple part get hard when I remembered his cool hand on my skin.

Then I moved my hand down to my tummy, and then down to where the hair begins, and when I rubbed myself around and around, I began to feel the dizzy kind of way I felt with Jeb when we were kissing and he undid my bra.

I don't know what made me stop then, but suddenly I got out of bed and went over to my dresser and picked up the picture I keep there of Daddy and Biscuit—the one I took when Daddy taught me how to use his Polaroid.

I stared at the picture real hard until I could see it clearly, and I remembered with so much sadness I could barely stand it what Daddy said to me that night about how I'd soon be learning to do lots of things for myself and how that was the meaning of growing up. The sadder I felt inside me, the heavier the picture felt in my hand.

I could feel tears coming, and I was afraid that if I began to cry really hard, I might drop the frame with Daddy and Biscuit's picture on the floor and it would be broken. So I sat down and put the picture in front of me on the rug.

As I stared at Daddy's face, something made me think of doing artificial respiration, as though maybe I could breathe life back into the picture so Daddy would come alive again. Suddenly I just needed to know what Daddy meant when he said soon I'd be doing lots of things for myself.

I remembered the fatherless family of deer I saw by Cedar Brook and felt angry at Daddy for not being with me anymore. Deer daughters don't need their fathers the way I needed mine. I couldn't figure out how I was going to get through Father's

Day at school next month, and graduation three years from now, and my wedding some day in the future, without my father being there.

The tears just started pouring out of my eyes, and I sat shivering and sobbing, feeling angry and abandoned and like life was completely and totally unfair.

Then I remembered the way Daddy looked the last time I saw him in the hospital, and the anger inside me began to soften. I realized then that Daddy didn't choose to die. It got easier not to be angry when I realized it wasn't Daddy's fault that he died.

I thought about how at some point this year I stopped playing the game of pretending Daddy wasn't really dead and that some day he'd come back to us all better again.

I guess that means I'm beginning to accept the fact that Daddy isn't ever coming back, because he can't come back, because he's dead. And death lasts forever.

I went over to my dresser and laid the picture of Daddy down flat so it wouldn't be facing me when I got back in bed.

Then I pulled the covers up and thought about Jeb. He just kind of sprang to life in my mind—so near and real. His funny mussy hair, the way he looks when he's running, his soft, sweet smile. I'd been with him yesterday morning. I knew we'd be together again soon.

I began to touch myself again, at first slowly and then faster and faster and then harder and harder until something amazingly exciting that had never happened before happened for the very first time. My body kind of lost control, but the feeling was a wonderful one, like a great, fast wave washing over me. I think it's what people mean when they say how sex is such a powerful experience.

When the dizzy, spinning feeling stopped, I thought of what it would feel like if Jeb did that to me. I realized then what grownups mean when they talk about how you have to be careful and hold back sometimes so you don't lose control. And then I fell asleep.

This morning I woke up remembering something I dreamed last night when I was sleeping. In the dream I'm running in a forest somewhere, and it's fall and getting cold like winter's coming soon. Leaves are falling all over the trail and piling up real high, and I have to kind of leap over them to get past them without falling or breaking stride as I run.

In the dream I'm running very fast and steady, and as I run the sound of my feet falling on the ground is pounding over and over again in my brain. With each footstrike the word "footfalls" hammers in my head, and I run on and on as if there is no end.

Young people learning to cope with the feelings and contradictions of growing up...

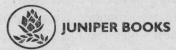 **JUNIPER BOOKS**